THE SWAN AND THE SERGEANT

THE SWAN AND THE SERGEANT

ALANA ALBERTSON

would like to share this book with another person, please purchase an additional copy for each recipient. If you're reading this book and did not purchase it, or it was not purchased for your use only, then please return to your favorite ebook retailer and purchase your own copy. Thank you for respecting the hard work of this author.

This book is dedicated to my late father, Joseph Chulick Jr.
I miss your brilliance, kindness, compassion, and laugh every day.

EPIGRAPH

"It is only with the heart that one can see clearly, for the most essential things are invisible to the eye."

— HANS CHRISTIAN ANDERSEN, THE UGLY DUCKLING

AUTHOR'S NOTE

To instantly get a free full length book, Deadly Sins, sign up for my newsletter: **Free Book**

Meet Bret! Though the ugly duckling is now a beautiful swan, the girl I fell in love with is long gone.

The Angel and The Rockstar

Inspired by Rumpelstiltskin

Meet Dax! All she has to do to destroy my life is to say my name.

The Maid and The Marine

Inspired by Cinderella

Meet Trace! I will never be her Prince Charming.

Rescue Me

Romantic Comedy Series

Doggy Style

Meet Preston! When it comes to doggy style, he's behind you 100%.

Blue Devils

Military Pilots Contemporary Series

Blue Sky

Meet Beckett! I'll never let down my guard for this Devil in a Blue Angel's disguise.

Blue Moon

Meet Sawyer: One Night with this Blue Devil will make you a sinner.

Blue Thunder

Meet Declan: Declan's back in town. Homecoming hero—local boy turned Blue Angel.

Se7en Deadly SEALs

Navy SEAL Romantic Thriller

Season One:

Conceit, Chronic, Crazed, Carnal, Crave, Consume, Covet

Season One Box Set

Meet Grant! She wants to get wild? I will fulfill her every fantasy.

Season Two:

Smug, Slack, Storm, Seduce, Solicit, Satiate, Spite

Meet Mitch! I'll always be your bad boy.

The Trident Code

Navy SEAL Romantic Suspense Series

Invincible

Meet Pat! I had one chance to put on the cape and be her hero.

Invaluable

Meet Kyle! I'll never win MVP, never get a championship ring, but some heroes don't play games.

Rescue Ranch

Navy SEAL Cowboys Series

Wild Love

Meet Chris! She shouldn't fall for the Navy SEAL next door.

Military Contemporary Stand Alone

Badass

Meet Shane! I'm America's cockiest badass.

(co-written with **Linda Barlow**)

Father Figure

Meet Gabriel! Forgive me, Father, for I have sinned.

(Co-written with **Jane Harvey-Berrick**)

$50,000 to appear on *Dancing with the Stars*.

$50,000 to humiliate myself on national television, lose my privacy, and become the laughingstock of the Marine Corps. But I can't say no. Not even if it means I have to face the woman who once destroyed me.

Ten years ago, reality star Selena Martinez was my dance partner and my girl. Though the self-professed ugly duckling is now a beautiful swan, the girl I fell in love with is long gone. Consumed with being a celebrity, her inner beauty has been replaced by an ugly lust for fame. When our coach offers me $5,000 a week to appear on TV's hot ballroom dance reality show, I have no desire to relive my painful past with

Selena, but I made a promise to my buddy that I'd take care of his wife and kids if he died on the battlefield.

One season, ten weeks, a small sacrifice to make for the man who saved my life.

Hand me my dance shoes.

I'm in.

(A version of this book was originally published as Love Waltzes In and Swing. This edition has been completely rewritten.)

AWARDS

Contest Awards for The Sergeant and The Swan

WINNER—Single Title 2012 RWA Golden Gateway

WINNER—Single Title 2012 RWA Heart of the West

WINNER—Single Title 2013 RWA Marlene

RUNNER UP—Single Title 2012 RWA Four Seasons

RUNNER UP—Single Title 2012 RWA Golden Rose

RUNNER UP—Classic 2008 RWA Stiletto

3rd PLACE—Single Title 2012 RWA Hot Prospects

BRET

AN-NU'MĀNĪYAH, IRAQ

I ripped open the care package from my mom. The contents tumbled out onto the tent's dirty floor—socks, lip balm, sunflower seeds, a magazine clipping, and a San Diego postcard.

Dear Bret,

I miss you very much. Benny asked me to send you this article. I really wish you would consider his offer. Please stay safe.

Love, Mom

I swallowed hard. A neon sticky pressed onto the wrinkled page had a message scrawled on it from my former master dance coach.

Bret, m'boy,
We'll make it worth your time.
Cheers, Benny

I barely recognized the sixteen-year-old boy in the magazine picture. My shoulder-length, wavy blond hair was slicked back, not shorn in a "high and tight" like my current haircut. There was no sign of the tattoos or muscles that currently defined my body. My golden skin stained from a bottle, not the harsh sun of Iraq.

My breath hitched at the sight of the other person in the photo. My arms were wrapped around a curvy young girl with long, wavy jet-black hair. The jade Latin gown she wore matched the color of her almond-shaped eyes.

Selena Martinez.

But now she was nothing like the sweet, awkward girl I had fallen in love with years ago. A quick skim of the page reaffirmed that for me, revealing a drop-dead gorgeous blonde posing in a bikini with a sultry pout on her heart-shaped face. If it wasn't for her eyes, I would swear it was a different woman.

Selena was now a reality star, a complete smoke show. Men around the world lusted after her. But for that one moment in time, she had been only mine.

I pushed her out of my mind, tossed the article aside, and removed the nine-mil pistol from my holster to clean it.

Lance Corporal Hernandez walked by me and snatched the page off my cot. After staring at it, Hernandez's face brightened.

"Hey, Staff Sergeant, this you?"

"No, it's my clone who's also named Bret Lord." I slid the rail back on my weapon and began disassembling it.

"You danced with Selena Martinez? Did you hit that?"

"Shut up, Hernandez or the one getting hit will be you —with the buttstock of my rifle." I grabbed the paper out of Hernandez's hands and smacked him on the side of the head. The kid didn't flinch.

"Staff Sergeant Twinkle Toes. Hey—can you hook me up with Selena? I'll be her boy toy. I love her. Man, she's smoking. Has the nicest ass. Not like all those skinny Russian chicks on that show." He nodded to himself with an eyebrow dancing. "Selena's on my list. She's Latina, too. We'd be perfect together. What was she doing with a *gringo* like you?"

The thought of a bunch of Marines jerking off to pictures of my first love made me sick. "Hernandez, you're way out of line." I reassembled my pistol.

"My bad, Staff Sergeant."

I grabbed the article, my pack, and my rifle. It was impossible to get some privacy in the tent. I could sit outside in a sandstorm—even that sounded like a welcome retreat from my immature men. I walked about five hundred feet, then plopped down in the hot sand.

The red sky hung above me, obscured by smoke from the nearby town. I struggled to catch a glimpse of the distant mountains. Sand seemed to pelt down from the heavens, blinding me and settling into every crevice in my body. I closed my eyes against the sting of the sand and turned my thoughts to Selena.

Was she the diva the tabloids made her out to be? Even after ten years, I could almost smell her buttery-coconut scent. A welcome change from the overflowing shitters, toxic diesel, and stench of my fellow Marines who hadn't bathed in three weeks.

The deep popping sound of shots from a nearby AK-47 roused my ears.

I stilled.

As a marksmanship instructor, I could distinguish the sound of any weapon system. These shots weren't the lighter, faster rounds of my men's M16s. Looking past the palm trees that peppered the dismal scene of dilapidated shacks, I tried to get a location on the origin of the gunfire. Probably just some insurgents outside of base. The rules of engagement were clear—I couldn't stop them from killing each other even if I wanted to. And I definitely wasn't going to endanger the lives of my men.

The sandstorm let up, and I reached into my pack to grab dinner. *Spaghetti with Meat and Sauce* was my favorite Meal, Ready-to-Eat, even if it did taste like chalk. Maybe I'd get lucky, and it would come with cinnamon apples for dessert. I opened the box and laid out the day's bounty: cherry-blueberry cobbler, potato sticks, wheat snack bread, plain cheese spread, lemon-lime beverage powder, and accessory pack "A": coffee, creamer, sugar, salt, Tabasco, a moist towelette, toilet paper, chewing gum, and matches.

I opened the cooking bag, placed the spaghetti pouch inside, filled it with water, and then leaned it against a rock to cook. Ha—here I was dining out of a pouch in hell, and Selena spent her days noshing at Michelin-starred restaurants.

I stared at the picture of Selena and me winning the U.S. National Youth Amateur Latin Ballroom Championship. Selena was now the star of the hit series *Dancing Under the Stars*. My childhood sweetheart was plastered on magazine covers, billboards, and advertisements. The details of my life back then had faded away from my memory. Being at war made everything a blur.

I took a swig of water from my CamelBak and downed two anti-malaria pills: one blue, one pink. The Marine Corps assured the troops that they were safe, but I'd bet the pills caused my daily headaches. Then again, maybe the migraines were just from the hundred-degree heat.

Staff Sergeant Ray Wilson emerged from the tent and sat beside me. Even though I wanted to be alone, I was happy to have my friend's company.

"Slim Jim?" Ray offered.

"Sure."

As I ripped the plastic off the snack, Ray nodded at the magazine article lying in the sand. "What's that all about?"

I grunted. "A month ago, my mom told me the judge on *Dancing* asked her if I would consider doing the show. He just sent me a note."

"For real?" Ray took a bite of his own Slim Jim. "You'd have to be stupid to give up this paradise of sand and gunfire for the mansions of Hollywood. Your mother does realize you're a Marine, right? You can't just leave the Corps and go on reality television."

"That's what I told her. But she has this crazy idea that the Marine Corps would let me do it for one season—like a recruiting tool. I doubt that, but I could use my vacation leave. Remember that kid on *American Pop Star*?"

"Yeah. Didn't he gain like thirty pounds and fail his PFT?" he snorted, and I shook my head.

"He did. But I'd be dancing eight hours a day—I'd be in even better shape."

He gestured up and down my frame with his Slim Jim.

Can you still dance, Patrick Swayze?"

"Good enough to teach some teen mom from MTV how to cha-cha. But I'd be the laughingstock of the Corps."

"Maybe not. I mean, you *are* the only Devil Dawg who happens to be a ballroom champion. You could be that all-American hero. The pretty face that recruits a load more boys to join the rest of us here and get shot at."

"If you think it sounds so great, I'll tell her *you'll* do it." I hated the public's obsession with the "celebrities" on those shows. Young kids who became millionaires for making sex tapes or wasting their days doing nothing but going to the gym, tanning, and partying. Influencers posting thirst traps on their social media. Meanwhile, my buddies and I were out here in hell, dodging bullets.

I checked my spaghetti. Done. I dug into the warm, gooey meal.

Ray shrugged. "The only dance I know is the latest TikTok, and something tells me I'd be more of a target for that than I am for being a Marine in Iraq."

"Ha." I had no desire to ever dance again. Once I joined the Corps, I had found my calling. "Nah, I'd rather stay here with my men. I wouldn't even consider it—if it weren't for Pierce."

Ray blinked hard. "What does the show have to do with Pierce?"

"I promised him that I'd take care of his family if anything happened to him. If I did the show, I could earn some money for them."

"Dawg, you'd do that for them? That would be crazy."

"He'd have done it for me." Pierce would've done anything for me. He had already proven that.

We sat there in silence.

Ray nodded toward me. "Pierce was a good dude. You should do it."

My hands were sticky with sweat. "I can't. I'd make a fool out of myself."

"Man, it wouldn't be that bad." Ray stretched out against a rock. "And you can go check out your ex-fiancée—she is *Maxim's* Sexiest Girl Alive. Even if she's with that pretty-boy dancer."

"Dima? That guy's a jerk. He was one of our coaches. But I would never get back together with Selena." Though she seemed sexier than ever, I had no desire to go there, not to the luscious curves of her breasts, the round globes of her ass, or golden waterfall of her hair.

A relationship between us could never work out. She was too focused on her career—always had been. Then again, I was married to the Marine Corps. I wouldn't allow myself to get tempted by the fame and money of Hollywood.

Ray rolled his eyes. "Well, you never know. Maybe she's changed." Ray broke out a bag of Skittles. "I'll go with you. Can you request Beyoncé as my partner?"

I laughed. "Not sure if Jay-Z would like that. Or your wife." Ray had one of the good ones. His wife was any Marine's dream. Beautiful and faithful, Nia raised their four children while Ray was away. She was the head of the Key Wives' Club, and still had time to send Ray the best care packages, hence his endless supply of Slim Jims.

After Selena, I vowed never to get close to anyone again, at least not until I left the Corps. I needed to focus on guiding my men—not get distracted wondering if another man was keeping my girl's bed warm while I fought a war thousands of miles away.

Ray stood up. "Nia'd be cool with it. She loves the show, man. Do it."

I didn't answer. I stuffed the article back into the pocket containing my "If I should die" letter.

The roar of more rounds boomed through the sky. Sweat soaked my cammies, weighing them against my chest. I couldn't see anything, but the rumbling of the helicopters overhead told me this was no training exercise.

I didn't say a word, but I knew what was about to go down. A fire built in my chest and adrenaline took over. Moments like this made all the sacrifices of war worth it—knowing my life meant something, and that I was responsible for not only protecting my men but also ensuring the safety of Americans back home. I tossed the rest of the food into my pack and gathered my weapons.

We leaped to our feet. We raced into the tent as if hounds were on our heels.

I screamed at my men. "Grab your weapons and take cover!"

Squinting at the bright lights, I slipped on my sunglasses even though I was still inside the airport terminal. Sunlight wasn't blinding me—it was the flashes from those horrible cameras.

"Back in one minute," my partner Dima said curtly and nodded to a nearby kiosk overflowing with souvenirs—leaving me at the mercy of the photographers.

A man thrust his microphone in my face. "Selena, are you coming back to *Dancing Under the Stars* next season?"

My seven-year contract didn't give me much choice. "If they want me back, I'll be there." That was all I could say. I was under strict orders not to reveal any details of the new season.

A female reporter dressed in a fitted suit pushed her way to the front of the mob. "Selena, is there any truth to the rumor that Dima had an affair with Poppy Mabel?"

I glared at Dima, who was surrounded by sunhats and adoring fans. His personal life off the dance floor was none of my business, but I wanted to make it clear that I wasn't the victim the tabloids painted me to be. "No. But if the rumors *were* true, there would be no scandal. Both Dima and Poppy are single." My eyes flicked to Dima. He took a break from posing for pictures with his fans and surged through the media swarm to pull me to his side.

"Poppy and me are the friends," he said. "The only woman in my life that I'm committed with is Selena." His accent always worsened when the media pressured him.

I narrowed my eyes at him, but he probably couldn't see them through my sunglasses. I'd seen the photos of Dima and Poppy frolicking at a pool in Vegas on the cover of a few magazines as we'd passed a newsstand at the entrance to the airport. It didn't bother me who he dated—as long as it didn't overshadow our purely *professional* partnership.

A young girl ran up to us, waving a promotional photo. "*Selima*! I just love you guys. I'm a competitive dancer, also. You're so amazing together! I hope you work things out and get married. The ballroom dream."

Selima—the tabloids' combined nickname for us—made me wince. Our identities were bound together even though we hadn't been romantically involved in years.

I took the photo. "All that matters is the dancing, dear. What's your name?"

"Amy."

I signed the photo. "Keep practicing those rumba walks, Amy. I hope to see you compete someday."

The girl squealed. "I just know you're going to win Blackpool this year. I'll be there!" Dima also signed her photo and gave her a kiss on the cheek.

We signed a few autographs, posed for more pictures, and answered questions for our fans.

After the crowd thinned out, we made our way to baggage claim.

"Welcome to San Diego, America's finest city," said a man holding a big sign bearing our names. Like we needed any more attention. He led us to a waiting limousine and lifted our bags into the trunk.

When I'd first met Dima, he would never let another man carry his luggage. Now he barely lifted a finger to do anything.

I took a deep breath as the limo swiftly moved away from the airport. We were there to defend our United States Professional Latin-American Title, and we'd also be followed by cameramen as they collected filler images for the new season of the show. If it were up to Dima, we would quit competing and capitalize on our celebrity status. But I wasn't about to let a television show get in the way of achieving my lifetime dream.

Not when I had given up everything for it.

Dima checked his phone, ignoring me now that the cameras were gone. Like always. Years ago, I'd idolized him. I was the young amateur, and he'd been the sexy dance god. Dima was a ballroom legend. He'd finaled at Blackpool with his former partner, Carrie. Twice. I never believed I'd be lucky enough to dance with him, especially since I had been such an awkward teen.

Until he transformed me.

Dima was also gorgeous—tall, black wavy hair, vibrant brown eyes. His deep Ukrainian accent used to drive me wild, the way his beautiful lips would say the word pleasure—*ple-e-shore.* But these days, all I saw was a Hollywood player with a freshly waxed chest.

Grateful to take a break from the dreary Los Angeles smog, I became mesmerized by the clear ocean. The aqua waves rippled in the distance as surfers dotted the coastline. I had never surfed. Dima forbade it. Why would I be so stupid to risk breaking my ankle to ride a break?

At least I could inhale the clean air.

"Selenichka, listen." Dima broke into my reverie to read out loud from his phone.

"'*Dancing Under the Stars* gains a new mystery dancer?'" Dima cocked his eyebrow at me, then focused back on his phone and read. "'Who's the newest male professional dancer to lace up his dancing shoes? Rumors have the cast in a frenzy wondering who will be the new dancer. Though normally the new professionals come from the troupe of backup dancers, the newest member of the cast has been recruited from a different field.'"

I rolled my eyes. "And?"

"And? Who it is?" Dima raised his phone. "No one has told to me nothing. No one on circuit has mentioned that they were asked to be on show."

I sighed. Today was not the day for speculating on rumors. We had too much to concentrate on to get worked up about who the new professional on the show might be.

"What do I think? I think it's probably someone we all know, maybe from another country. Or from the UK version? And gossip columnists also have nothing better to do than make stuff up. If you're so worried, ask Benny."

"You're right. I'll ask to him." He frantically texted a message.

The limo rolled onto Harbor Drive. Cherry blossoms scented the air. As we approached the Coronado Bridge, a humongous Navy carrier slid underneath.

My breath hitched.

Was Bret on that ship?

I shook my head. It didn't matter. We hadn't spoken in years and likely would never speak again.

The limo pulled in front of the Sheraton San Diego. The bellman strode over to assist the driver with our luggage. I didn't have time to wait for Dima to check us in. "I have to hurry to the spa, and then Benny asked me to run through some quick choreography for the show. I'll text you later." I kissed him on the cheek, grabbed my shoe bag, jumped out of the car, and rushed to the hotel spa.

But I *wanted* to turn and chase after the limo and hitch a ride to the beach. No more fresh air and cherry blossoms for me. From this moment until the competition, it would be all business. Competition eve was always a headache, with all the tanning, makeup, hair, fasting.

The calming scent of lavender filled the reception area. I closed my eyes and smiled. Hotel spas were my standard primp spots for competitions. The staffs were thorough and professional. Even better, they were nice. I could stand a good dose of nice before I walked into that den of dancing wolves. A competition dance floor was no place for the weak or the unprepared.

"Selena Martinez, here for my ten-fifteen appointment."

"Oh yes, Miss Martinez. We're so thrilled to have you." The receptionist consulted her computer screen. "You're scheduled for a facial, a Brazilian bikini wax, a brow wax, a Mandarin Orange Body Polish followed by a custom sparkle spray tan, and then you'll receive a mani and pedi while Alberto touches up your roots and tightens your hair extensions." She abandoned the screen and leaned forward, her eyes wide. "You know, Miss Martinez, I just love *Dancing Under the Stars*— really, it's my favorite show. You ballroom dancers must lead such glamorous lives."

I pressed my lips into a forced smile. "Yes. We're so blessed. And please, call me Selena."

I sat on the sofa and thought about my "glamorous" life. I lived in the gym and the studio, sometimes dancing up to eight hours a day. Every weekend was spent in a hotel in some random state, competing. My diet consisted of egg whites, vegetables, soup, and salad. I couldn't even eat fruit—too much sugar. And I hadn't had a weekend off in two years.

The paparazzi stalked me. No man had the guts to ask me out, knowing that his picture would be a *TMZ* headline if we were ever caught together. I couldn't even take my trash cans out of my house in my sweats for fear that I'd get photographed. I hated all the nonsense I had to endure to dance.

What if I'd chosen a different path all those years ago?

It didn't matter.

I'd probably never get married and have a family.

But enough of the self-pity. I did love my life. How blessed was I? The older generation of ballroom dancers had spent every penny they earned on competing. The show allowed me to pursue my dream of winning Blackpool while not having to worry about money.

For years, I had struggled. My mother had worked three jobs and cleaned dance studios at night in exchange for my lessons. I was finally in a position to support my family. My first big splurge had been buying my mom a condo and starting a college fund for my younger sister.

Now I could make twenty thousand dollars just for appearing at a party. Dima and I had even started our own charity, bringing ballroom classes to inner-city kids. I was so appreciative of the opportunities the show had given me. How lucky was I to make a living out of my true passion? I lived to dance. I chastised myself for even feeling ungrateful for a second when so many people struggled.

But deep in my heart, I knew what I'd given up to have this life could never be replaced.

I had only opened a magazine to the first page when the receptionist called over to me. "Selena, Larissa is ready for you."

I sucked in a deep breath before standing. *Let the games begin.*

In the backroom, I stripped off my peach-colored terry sweatsuit, put on a smock, and lay on the paper-covered table.

Larissa entered the room and gave me a smile. "I just got tickets to the competition tomorrow. I can't wait to see you win."

"Thank you for supporting us."

She painted the hot wax onto my skin. "Are you thinking of retiring? I read in *Star Magazine* that you want to start a family."

Larissa ripped the hair from above my eye, but the face I made had nothing to do with the pain. *Star*, of course.

"I hope to someday." I yearned to take a break and start a family. I was confident that I'd be able to balance my career and children, but I hadn't been on a date in years. People outside of the industry didn't realize that no one could ever have a healthy relationship in the ballroom world.

Dancers had three options for dating: they could date their partner and combine their floor and relationship problems, like what had happened with Dima and me; they could date a dancer who was not their partner, and the worse dancer of the two would be jealous of the other's success; or they could date a non-dancer, who usually had a hard time understanding the partner relationship and the travel demands.

How would I explain to a prospective boyfriend that I spend ten weeks twice a year training celebrities? In the show's off-season, I spend every weekend in a hotel in different states or countries with Dima at some random competition. Add in my celebrity status, with cameras following me everywhere, and it was too much drama for most men to handle.

So, basically, it was hopeless.

A lump gathered in my throat. *No nerves.*

Larissa paused, a new glob of pink wax on the stick in her hand. "Well, you guys just look so good together. Watching you two dance is amazing. It's too bad about all the rumors going around. It can't be easy on a couple...right?"

Maybe that was why I couldn't get a date. Everyone still thought I was involved with Dima. "We aren't a couple. We just dance together."

"Oh, I'm sorry." Larissa cleaned up my other eyebrow. "Okay, honey, time for your bikini."

I spread my legs.

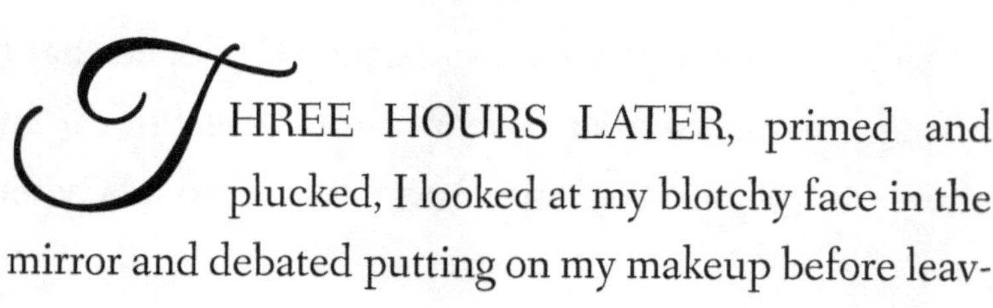

THREE HOURS LATER, primed and plucked, I looked at my blotchy face in the mirror and debated putting on my makeup before leaving. Forget it—it would just sweat off in rehearsal. Though my natural hair color was a beautiful espresso brown, it currently was bleached blonde, which shined great onstage under the bright lights but in plain sunlight resembled straw. Dima forced me to dye it because he thought it would make a better contrast to his own dark hair.

I had no ability to express myself—I was a product.

I pulled my long brittle locks back into a tight ponytail, grabbed my oversized purse filled with my dance shoes, and exited the spa. Putting my sunglasses on, I headed over to the small ballroom to meet one of the producers.

"Selena Maria Martinez."

The deep voice stopped me from taking another step. There was only one person who would use my middle name.

But it couldn't be him.

Maybe I had fantasized so many times that he'd found me that I was now imagining his voice. Yup, that was it. I was totally losing it.

There was no way Bret Lord could be inches away from me.

Unless . . .

I slowly turned.

Oh my God!

Bret Lord stood in front of me.

He wore khaki pants and a white polo shirt that hugged his ripped chest. A few hairs peeked out of the neckline, teasing me. Surrounded by groomed dancers and Hollywood pretty boys, I hadn't seen a real man's chest in years.

For the past ten years, I'd dreamt of him but never could see his face.

My mind raced.

"Bret! What are you doing here?" I thought for a second that he was going to hug me, but he just crossed his arms, holding a shoebox, which seemed odd.

I was grateful that the sunglasses hid the guilt behind my eyes.

Ten years ago, he had been given orders to some base in North Carolina. I'd sent him a final letter during boot camp, ending our engagement.

Such a coward, I hadn't even shown up at his graduation to tell him in person. I couldn't bear to face him because I had already made my painful decision, and there was no way I could ever reverse it.

I'd never heard from him again. He'd vanished from my life. Not even a Facebook or Instagram account I could stalk. All I could do was occasionally scour the Internet, looking for the names of casualties in the military. I'd breathe easier after not seeing his name. For a while, at least.

He opened his mouth to reply, but I blurted out, "Are you still in the Marines?"

Bret's blue eyes blinked hard. "Yes. I won't retire for ten more years."

"I can't believe it's really you."

Finally, Bret stepped forward, one arm extended as if showing some affection was an obligation. I returned the gesture. The shoebox that Bret clutched forced space between us, like an invisible line. My cheeks stretched into a thin smile, one meant to lessen some of the pressure around us.

He released me, and I pushed up my sunglasses on my head so I could study him. Was this gorgeous man really the same scrawny teenage boy to whom I'd lost my virginity? His hair was cut short, his skin a deep brown that no tanning bed could achieve. The bottom of a U.S.M.C. tattoo was visible from his sleeve. Though Bret kept his distance, his minty scent filled the air. His lips curved into that lazy grin of his.

He was sexier than any movie star I had met over the years. The thought of being with a real man, muscles sculpted from carrying weapons, not practicing Pilates, made me quiver.

I glanced down at his left hand. No ring. The breath I'd been holding escaped.

"I almost didn't recognize you, blondie. You look great, Sel."

I shuddered. I was in my sweats without so much as a tinted moisturizer or lip gloss, and he thought I looked great? If Dima saw me now, he would scold me about my appearance.

I glanced down for a moment before meeting his gaze with renewed confidence. "Nationals are here tomorrow. Are you sticking around?"

"Wasn't planning on it." He gave a half-smile. "You've been to one competition; you've been to them all."

I nodded. That was expected. But I hoped he would agree to hang out with me, even for a little bit. Though I knew that he had no reason to. He hated me. And with good reason.

I cleared my throat. "Maybe we can grab a drink tonight? To catch up."

Bret took out his phone, his thumbs moving across the virtual keyboard. "I'd love to Sel, but I have plans."

Plans? Was he still upset after all these years about the way I had ended our engagement? Probably. I had been such a bitch. *Of course* he wouldn't want to hang out with me. But he had no idea what had happened. Well, that was my fault. I never told him. I couldn't tell him. He would kill Dima if he knew.

And I hated to admit it, but I was almost shocked that he'd told me no. No one told me no anymore. I was so used to people fawning over me, that Bret's rejection stunned me.

Who was I kidding? I didn't deserve him after what I'd done.

My cheeks burned with fresh guilt. A hollow pain radiated in my chest. Ten years of wondering, imagining, dreaming of our reunion, and all I got was a weak hug? I couldn't even get my first love to have a casual drink with me. And let's be real—I didn't just want to hang out with him. I wanted to spend the night with him. He was gorgeous.

I bit my lip and shrugged my shoulders. "I get it. Well, it was nice seeing you again."

Benny Brooks snuck up behind us. "Bret, m'boy. Great to see you again. I see you've reacquainted yourself with Selena—why don't you both come inside, and we can get started."

Get started? What was going on?

Bret fidgeted. "I have to dance...with her?"

Benny's lips turned upwards into a devilish grin. He opened the doors to the ballroom. "Selena, I want you to partner Bret for his tryout."

Tryout? What the hell?

A thud echoed against the floor. My purse lay at my feet, and I scrambled to pick it up again. "Benny, uhm, you never said it was a tryout. You said you just needed to borrow me to run through choreography?"

"Sorry, sweetie. I thought it would be best if you dance with Bret for his audition. I'm sure you've heard the rumors that we're hiring a new professional this season. A true-blue United States Marine! The audience will love him. They're sick of seeing all the foreign wankers. And since you used to be his sheila, I thought it would be easier for him to dance with you."

Bret grimaced. "Whatever you say, Benny." Bret walked into the ballroom, sat on a chair, and took some dancing shoes out of the box.

"Tryout? Uhm, of course, Benny. No problem. I didn't know Bret was dancing again or like ever." My gaze darted over to Bret only for a moment. "But of course, you'd be lucky to have him on the show. He is...I mean, was, an amazing dancer."

Could I speak in coherent sentences? That was a definite no.

I sat on a chair on the opposite side of the room from Bret and started attacking the soles of my shoes with my shoe brush, pieces of suede flying in the air.

Despite my childhood dream of Bret and I making a life together, I hadn't been able to turn down Dima's partnership offer. I had made an agonizingly difficult decision. Now, I was exactly where I'd hoped to be in my career.

But I'd never expected Bret would be sitting in the same room, waiting to dance with me again.

Iaced up my dance shoes. What was I doing? I couldn't dance with Selena again —no matter how good she looked, how good she smelt. I knew the producers would throw us together. I just didn't think it would be this soon.

Pierce's little boy's face flashed in my mind. When I'd stopped in to see him on my way here, he'd been so grateful. But the house had been falling apart, the garden overgrown, and if I hadn't already been given approval from the Marine Corps to take this chance, I'd have quit then and there—just to make that kid smile.

But I could do better by earning this money for him and his family.

Too bad I had to burn through two years of personal vacation time to do the show. I had one shot at convincing the executive producer of *Dancing Under the Stars* that I was the right man for the job.

I was perfect on paper—a decorated United States Marine, an American Ballroom Champion—but could I still dance? I'd have to prove myself.

Seeing Selena...it threw me. I hadn't counted on seeing her so soon and definitely hadn't expected to touch her and smell her. She looked so hot, all natural and not painted up. The thought of running my hands all over her curvy body made me lose focus. I wasn't prepared to be this close to her so soon.

I walked over to Benny. My former master coach looked just like I'd remembered: tall, silver-haired, with just a hint of sleaze. Ballroom's very own Crocodile Dundee. An icon in the dance world, Benny was a six-time Blackpool champion, winning twice with each of his first three wives. His fourth and current wife, *Dancing Under the Stars* professional dancer Vika, was a twenty-four-year-old Ukrainian knockout who was also Dima's cousin.

Benny stretched out his hand, his blood-orange silk suit shimmering with the movement. His hair was the same color as the sterling silver in his black jade bolo tie.

Benny held out his hand. "This is just a formality. I told the other producers that a better man never stood in two dance shoes. Your blood's worth bottling. It would be an honor to have a hero on our show."

I cleared my throat. I never knew how to respond to someone calling me a hero. "Thank you, Benny, for giving me the opportunity. It's great to see you again."

The doors flew open, and I was overtaken by the spicy smell of strong perfume. Karen Brooks Lopez stormed in. Karen was a two-time Blackpool Latin Champion with Benny, her first husband. They had two children together, Nicole and Jared. Then Karen shocked the dance world by leaving Benny when she was thirty, at the peak of her career, for her eighteen-year-old student, Carlos Lopez.

Karen trained Carlos, and eventually, they won Blackpool, stealing the title from Benny and his second wife. Karen had a reputation for being a diva, demanding limousines, and five-hundred-thread-count sheets. She and Carlos spent all of their energy training their own little devil spawn, Gregory Lopez, a brilliant rising star in the amateur Latin world.

Karen took my face in her hands and kissed my cheeks. "Bret, wow. You have turned into a sexy man." She ran her fingers over my biceps, and I flinched.

"Hi, Karen. You look beautiful as always." I kissed her hand and then stepped aside to create some distance between us.

"Oh, Bret. I can see you're still the charmer. I'll tell Carlos to watch out—I might have found my next husband. Need to catch up to Benny." She laughed. Her cackle reminded me of the screaming golden jackals in Iraq.

Benny rubbed his temples. "Are we done? We have a show to cast. Don't mind her, Bret; she's got kangaroos loose in the top paddock."

I laughed. I always loved Benny's funny Australian slang.

Karen playfully smacked my butt. Yup, she hadn't changed a bit. "Well, I'm ready for a show." Her fake, plump lips curled, and she flashed me a smile.

I made my way to Selena. My body clenched—I was actually nervous to touch her. Seeing her made me feel like a teenager all over again.

Selena's green eyes seemed almost dazed. "I never thought I'd dance with you again."

"Neither did I."

It was now or never.

I reached my hand out to her. She was ridiculously hot but looked nothing like I had remembered. My girl had been self-conscious, shy, and awkward. Her long dark hair had been wavy, shiny, and lush. I missed the girl I had fallen in love with.

Selena's skin glowed, showing off the freckles that were always airbrushed out in the magazines. Her hair was pulled off her face as if she had just emerged from the shower, a vision I was trying to push out of my mind.

I ran my hand through my own hair. "I didn't expect to run into you today. I wanted to make the show on my own, without any favors."

"It's not a favor. I'm thrilled to partner you. I never even thought I'd see you again." She bit her lip, took my hand, and got into position. "Ready?"

"Absolutely." I forced a smile but couldn't look her in the eyes for more than a second. No matter how strong

I was today, seeing her made my heart ache over how she had destroyed me.

After I'd returned from Iraq, my mom had started training me in secret. She was still a dance instructor and had rented a small studio in Oceanside to help me since I was stationed in nearby Camp Pendleton. I'd adopted Banjo, a pug/lab mix from the shelter on base, and every day after work, I would practice, then spend most nights escaping with Banjo to the dog beach to relax. Well, that and try to teach Banjo to turn off the lights, open the refrigerator, and fetch me a beer.

Being back on American soil, spending nights staring out at the clear ocean, I had regained my sanity and made peace with my time in Iraq. I had also enjoyed my last days of anonymity.

Now, my moment of truth had come.

Benny turned on the music. "How about a foxtrot?"

George Michael's voice began singing "Feeling Good."

I pulled Selena into my arms, just like old times. "Sounds good." I adjusted her into a classic foxtrot hold.

Selena leaned her body against mine as I swayed her back and forth. We took a few basic steps, and I led her into promenade. I turned my head toward her and held her gaze this time. On the dance floor, all insecurities faded away. I was in control.

We had been "America's Ballroom Sweethearts," the entire industry pinning its hopes on our backs like a million targets. Our career was mapped out for us, with sponsors who funded our travel, our coaching expenses, our costumes. We'd been the future of DanceSport.

But I had wanted to do something honorable with my life, and she had initially supported my decision to enlist. And at the time, it had been a practical decision. Back then, there was no future in ballroom dancing. No television shows, no outside endorsements, no way to support a wife and family.

She said she'd wait for me, but by the time I'd graduated from boot camp, she was long gone.

She left me for Dima.

Her thumb hooked over my right bicep as we merged together. The thump of her heartbeat vibrated off my chest, just like the first night we had made love. It wasn't right, to get caught up in the past like this, to remember her this way. But dancing had a way of doing that, grabbing on to any weak flame and igniting it.

I took charge and guided her through the steps. We flowed around the floor.

After two laps, Benny changed the song. George was now singing "Jesus to a Child."

"Rumb-a, please," Benny called out.

My fingers traced over Selena's wrist. We began to dance a slow, soulful rumba.

Our rumba.

I pushed her away and led her into an overturned back break, and then pulled her back into me. My hands dropped around her tiny waist, and our hips melded together. Her body moved with mine, perfectly in sync. We had once danced as a boy and a girl. Now, we danced as a man and a woman. The back of my hand brushed her neck. A lock of hair fell on her cheek. My fingers traced down her body.

"I missed you," she whispered as she wrapped her leg around me.

Missed me? She left me while I was away for three months, and before I'd even had a chance to chase her, she had run off to dance with Dima.

I'd missed *her* plenty—all those lonely nights of boot camp. Every time I got my ass handed to me by the drill instructors, thinking of her had given me a reason to push forward.

At first, she wrote me weekly, then the letters tapered off. She then sent me a final letter, ending our engagement, and telling me she had returned her ring to my mother.

When she didn't show up at my graduation, I'd pushed her out of my mind. It had worked for a while —until she started popping up on television and every newsstand in the country. Deployment had at least meant an end to the constant torture of seeing her face on television, except even worse pinups of her were on many of my men's walls.

I pressed my lips to her ear, but no sound came out. I placed my hand on her lower back and dipped her to the floor.

Benny cut off the music.

"Ace! Bravo, mate. You haven't lost your step. I told the suits as much. What do you think, doll?"

Selena pulled away from me. "It's as if he never quit."

Benny conferred with Karen, acting like professionals, not ex-spouses. Karen laughed at something Benny was saying. Selena and I stood there, both keeping our gazes upfront.

But even though I was a trained Marine, I couldn't keep my attention at front. I stole a glance at Selena. She had been so warm against me just a few minutes ago.

Maybe I should try to seduce her. She'd asked me to have a drink with her, but I said no, and she told me she missed me. What kind of dumbass was I? She was perfection.

But she belonged in my past.

I'd been wrong before. It wasn't dancing that was awkward as hell. It was this, the aftermath.

Benny turned and smiled. "Welcome to *Dancing Under the Stars*! I told them the other day—I said he's the good oil. Surer than a bum in the bucket. The others thought you might have lost your touch. I said,

'Not unless the Sahara freezes over and the camels come home with skates on.'"

Karen kissed me smack on the lips and rubbed her nails through my hair.

I was so thrilled that I squeezed her waist without a thought.

I'd done it. Everything had fallen into place. I'd have enough money to help out Pierce's family.

"Congrats, Bret." Selena embraced me. "I can't wait to work with you this season."

My mouth stretched wide, and I was seized with the urge to hold her again. But I couldn't let myself go there, ever. I could never trust Selena.

I should thank her for making me look good on the floor. A dancer was only as good as his partner, and despite her shock over seeing me without warning, she'd held her own. I mean, why wouldn't she? She was the best dancer in the world.

But she was already looking away, so I aimed my grin at Benny and Karen instead, extending a hand. "Thank you, Benny, Karen. I won't disappoint you."

"I'm sure you won't. We have some details to go over with the contract." Benny addressed Selena. "Thanks, doll. We won't need you anymore."

She twirled a lock of her hair. "You sure? I can stay and give him some pointers if you like."

Benny shooed her away. "I know you have to get ready for tomorrow. You can shoot through."

"Okay. Bye, Bret." She turned toward me and gave me another quick hug. "See you soon." She removed her shoes, placed them in her bag, put her sunglasses back on, and walked out of the ballroom. The door slammed behind her.

"Don't fret about her—she'll be apples. Now, tomorrow night, we have a crew ready to take some footage for your introduction on the show," Benny said as he rifled through his briefcase.

"Tomorrow? At the competition?" I didn't want to watch Selena compete. At least, not with Dima. Seeing that slimy motherfucker put his hands all over her would make me ill. He had been our teacher— Dima had groomed her. It wasn't right.

"Well, you must lob in. You'll get to mingle with most of the cast. There's also a surprise for you."

A surprise? Dancing with Selena was enough of a surprise. What else was Benny plotting? "I'll be there."

Benny rattled on about schedules, media appearances, and payment plans as Karen ogled me. I might've been able to pay attention to what Benny was saying had it not been for Selena's lingering coconut scent on my skin.

*L*oud booms caused the floor to vibrate. I followed the bass path to the sound system, where I found Dima dressed in a flashy Armani suit. I almost tripped over him. Not that he'd notice with his gaze set on Elizabeth, his latest blonde-haired, blue-eyed, baby-faced prodigy, and the youngest professional dancer on the show at only eighteen. Dima had discovered her at a studio in Utah and recommended that Benny cast her on the show.

"Excuse me..." I interrupted.

"Hi, Selena," Elizabeth said. "Dima was, uhm, he was just going over some steps with me. Good luck tonight. I'll see you inside." Then she ducked away.

Dima leaned on the pillar next to him and smiled. "Ready to win, *Zaika*?"

I winced. Though I'd once been quite fond of his cute nickname for me, a word that meant rabbit, hearing him use it now made me want to hop away. "Found out who the mystery dancer is." I teased.

He glared at me. "Who it is?"

"It's Bret."

Dima's back straightened, temples bulging. "Bret . . . Lord?"

"Yup. Isn't that crazy?"

His hand tightened into a fist. "I don't understand. Isn't he in the war? He hasn't danced together with anyone in years."

I took a step back, crossing my arms. "He's still with the Marines. I'm as confused as you are. Benny asked me to partner him in his tryout."

"How did he dance together with you?"

"He was incredible, actually." I watched the jealous reaction on Dima's face and enjoyed it. Maybe we will use that anger tonight in our Paso.

His lips curled. "That's ridiculous." He tapped his foot. "It do not matter. We need to focus now." He squeezed my hand. "Remember, we are nothing without each other."

Dima loved me in his own way, I knew that. But our love had always been toxic.

Jenny Ming walked over to us. "Selena, we have to leave now." Jenny's pale face flushed red, her eyes darting at Dima. Her hatred toward him was an open secret. She was clutching my makeup case. "You still have to gossip with the judges, and I have to sew you into your costume and do your makeup."

I hated talking to the judges. Picturing their faces caused that fluttery sensation in my stomach that I got before every competition.

I exhaled. "Let's do this."

Jenny, who was also on *Dancing Under the Stars*, competed in Standard, not Latin, so we could always help each other get ready. Tonight was my night, and Jenny rushed about, making sure everything went as planned.

Dima hooked my arm and led me inside the ballroom, with Jenny trailing behind us.

We made our grand entrance. Before *Dancing Under the Stars* was on television, competitions had been low-key events, relegated to the ballrooms of hotels. These days, when one of the dancers on the show competed, a red carpet was rolled out, and *TMZ* cameras were in our faces.

We all smiled for the cameras, gave a few autographs to our fans, and headed into the ballroom. After waltzing through the luxurious lounge, we walked over to the cramped vendor room. We made our way through the maze of stage jewelry, ballroom shoe peddlers, photographers, and costume designers.

Jenny headed over to the registration table and checked us in. Even though people were paying the organizers to come to see the competitors dance, all competitors still had to buy tickets to the event.

The Latin music playing in the ballroom overtook me, and I swayed to the beats of cha-cha. I scanned the ballroom for familiar faces and breathed a sigh of relief after reassuring myself that Bret wasn't lurking around. The last thing I needed was to be distracted by him tonight.

The thought of him made me impossibly hot. Had he felt what I had when we had danced? Dima was technically perfect, but with Bret, it was different. My body reacted to his touch, my soul to his.

What was he doing on the show anyway? How on earth did Benny convince him to be on the show?

Ay, I couldn't think about him. Not tonight.

Jenny returned from the desk and handed us our tickets. "Go schmooze, Sel. I'll get set up for you in the dressing room. See you in fifteen." She hugged me and then rushed off to set up my costumes and makeup.

Dima and I did our rounds and kissed up to the judges in the house. Dima flirted with Karen, as her son, Jared, chatted up Elizabeth. Elizabeth's partner, Ricardo, only had eyes for Mikey, his young boyfriend.

His arm was wound tightly around his wife. Vika's platinum hair was slicked into a sparkly bun, gold earrings framing her face and violet eyes glinting. She looked like an angel. Dima had introduced her to Benny at a competition in Moldova. Benny had certainly given her the life, plucking her from her small village in the Ukraine, training her to be his protégée, forcing his son to be her partner, casting her on the show.

Vika walked toward me and leaned in for a cheek kiss. "Selenichka, you look beautiful to me. Good luck to you tonight."

"*Chacibo*, Vika. I love your dress. Good luck to you." Endless seasons on a show together could turn anyone into close friends. This cast of characters was my family. I had no life outside of these people. This world.

"Ahh, Selena. You look stunning, lassie. Let me have a gander." Benny moved toward me.

I steadied my nerves. I was unfortunately used to being leered at by old men. "Thanks, Benny. You must be thrilled to see Vika and Jared compete tonight."

"Yes, luv, it's great to see them give it a fair go." He wet his lips and whispered in my ear, "But we both know they're a no-hoper against you and Dim'er. Sorry about earlier with Bret. I wanted to give him the best chance and knew you would try to knock back if I told you ahead of time."

I smiled, glad for his vote of confidence. "It's fine. I was just shocked. I'm glad he's going to be on the show. How did you convince him to be on it?"

Benny's face dropped. "Well, it's tragic, really. His friend was killed in Iraq. He is trying to raise money for his family."

Oh my god! My heart ached. How awful. And what a saint Bret was. I was truly a moron for ever leaving him.

Nicole and her husband, Eric, walked over to the group.

Nicole kissed Benny. "Hi, Daddy. Hi, Selena. Are you excited about tonight?" Nicole cradled their infant daughter.

I was in awe of Eric and Nicole, one of the only couples in the ballroom world who were truly in love, on and off the floor. "Hi, Nikki. I'm thrilled. Thanks for helping me with my cha-cha choreography."

"No worries." Nicole placed baby Rebecca in Eric's arms.

A pang clutched my belly. Would I ever have a family of my own?

I took out my phone and looked at the time. "I have to run and get ready."

"Me, too." Vika gave Benny a kiss on the cheek, and he patted her bottom.

Nicole took Vika's bag from her father and smiled at him. "Let's go."

I would never understand how it didn't bother Nicole that her stepmother was ten years younger than she was.

Elizabeth joined us, and we walked down the hallway together. We posed for a few fan pictures for the younger dancers. Visions of my twelve-year-old self squealing after receiving a kiss on the cheek from champion twenty-two-year-old Dima flooded my head.

"Selena, about time." Jenny's voice rang out as I walked through the door. That girl couldn't whisper if her life depended on it.

Jenny stood before a single-mirrored makeup table. She helped me get into my costume. After giving up on my stubborn dress straps, Jenny settled into gluing crystals above my eyebrow so quickly that it looked like someone had hit fast-forward on the scene in front of the mirror.

Nicole led Vika over to a corner and unfastened her bun. Elizabeth's sisters helped her get ready. At least ten other dancers were in various stages of undress. Another dancer bound her long black hair into a knotted ponytail on the top of her head, like an Arabian princess. One dancer rubbed baby oil on her body; another was being sewn into her costume.

The door flew open, startling everyone. The rancid smell of yesterday's Stroganoff wafted into the room.

"Lovely, the Russian Mafia is here," Jenny muttered. She threw a look of pity Vika's way then buried her head in my bag, looking for God knows what. Nicole excused herself to go check on her baby.

Vika's grandmother Irina and her six-person entourage took over the dressing room. Irina and two pre-pubescent Ukrainian dancers started spreading Vika's costumes in the cramped right corner of the room. Vika stripped down to nothing but her dance heels.

"Vika, *sidyat!*" Irina grabbed a still-naked Vika by her hair and shoved her into a chair to finish her makeup as her ladies-in-waiting fussed with her nails and jewelry.

Vika had married Benny to get a green card. Dima had also married his first partner for a green card, and he'd tried for years to get his cousin over here legally. In the end, he'd set her up with Benny.

Benny adored her, but I doubted that Vika truly loved him in any way other than a father figure.

Vika's family bullied her into competing, teaching long hours at their studio, showcases, and keeping up appearances. Dima used to drill into my brain that this lifestyle was a privilege, and Americans like me didn't know how to sacrifice. But then, he got famous. To Vika, happiness was a blend of success and wealth. She had told me as much.

But Vika's eyes told another story.

So did mine.

Jenny glued on my mink fur eyelashes with rhine-stones on the tips and rubbed on a final coat of Pro-Tan and Sun Shimmer to make my skin gleam. Then she started on my makeup: eyes brushed with rainbow-iridescent shades of a peacock, cheeks stained blood-red, and lips painted the color of cotton candy.

Yakking with the judges had cost me precious preening time. I shoved my hair into a sequined headband. Through the mirror, I stole a glance at Vika in her smoking-hot gown. It was completely nude underneath, with a sheer slip and hand-sewn rhinestones that adorned her body, with pink Swarovski crystals covering her ta-tas and, as Benny would say, her "Map of Tasmania." From a distance, she would appear to be dancing naked.

"Okay, Selena. You look beautiful as usual." Jenny gave me a hug. "You're going to do great."

"Thanks, Jen."

"Will the couples in Heat One of the Closed Professional United States Latin Championship please make their way to the on-deck area?" a voice with a British accent beckoned over the intercom.

I fluffed out my extensions and ran out into the hallway.

"Selena!" Dima yelled from inside the ballroom.

I raced into the ballroom and stood by his side. He kissed me on the forehead. I took a second to straighten the number on his back. Facing the audience, my gaze swept the room randomly—until it zeroed in on Bret, standing by the bar with a beer in his hand.

Holy shit.

He wore a sleek black suit and a conservative blue tie that matched his eye color, which I had adored years ago. Looking like a shiny boot in the sea of rhinestone dresses and flashy suits surrounding him, he didn't seem to care how out of place he was in my world of glitter and glam, a world that used to be part of his daily life.

He stared off somewhere to the left, and my eyes blurred on him. Why was he suddenly everywhere? And why was I always the last to know?

Many years ago, Bret and I won this competition together, our first big win. So far, no other night had been able to rival the elation I'd experienced on that one. The more time passed, the more I reminisced about the happiest night of my life. I had achieved my goal with the boy I loved, and we had a bright future planned together. More importantly, I'd felt safe and secure, a feeling I'd been grasping to get back ever since.

A sharp tug at my hand and an even sharper glare from Dima brought me back to the present. Dima was my partner now, my life, even if we weren't romantically involved. I needed to push Bret out of my mind so I could win. After all, I had sacrificed my soul and happiness to become a champion.

I took one last look Bret's way, hoping maybe he had vanished. But our eyes met. Bret winked at me.

I blew a kiss back. I was in costume—I could excuse my flirtation as part of the show.

I had to dance my heart out tonight to show Bret how far I'd come as a dancer. Maybe then he'd realize I made the right decision, many years ago, to leave him and my heart behind.

Maybe I'd be able to convince myself too.

BRET

So far, the competition hadn't been as painful as I had thought it would be. The producers filmed a segment with me talking about being at my first competition in over ten years. It was better than dodging land mines in the desert, that was for sure.

I clutched my beer bottle and headed into the ballroom for the final round. The bright lights reflected off the rhinestones, blinding me. After regaining sight—my eyes fell on Selena in the on-deck area.

Dima came from behind her and took her hand. The eleven judges strutted around the floor in formation like Marines in boot camp. The female judges displayed no emotion, probably from all that Botox they were always shooting their faces with. The sweat-filled room reeked of fake tanning spray and ripe feet.

"Ladies and gentlemen," the announcer said. "We are now going to proceed with the final round of the Closed Professional International Latin Championship. The judges have recalled the following six couples to the final round. From California, Couple 187—Dmitri Volkov and Selena Martinez."

The crowd erupted in applause. Dima led her to the floor, and Selena's eyes scanned the audience, landing right on me. It was like she could feel my intense stare always falling back on her.

She was definitely flirting with me—how could I resist the most beautiful woman in the world?

She wore a yellow-fringed dress that was open on the side, revealing her perfectly toned body—a far cry from the conservative black dresses she used to compete in when we were teens. She had always been so self-conscious about her body back then, though I had always thought she was perfect.

I sat at a round table and surveyed the crowd. Never had I thought I'd be back at a dancing competition, sitting amongst the spectators, pretending that I hadn't once been part of the show. How could I never have realized how gaudy this whole scene was? Both female and male dancers committed immigration fraud and married people they didn't love just to stay in America. Older women paid tens of thousands of dollars for costumes and lessons to compete with younger professional male dancers, who doubled as gigolos. To think of how much good that money could do for injured Marines and their struggling families... The whole dance world made me sick.

This time it would be different. Instead of heartache and broken toes, I planned to leave the season with enough money to change the life of my friend's family.

After another swig of my beer, I relaxed in my seat. It was showtime.

Time to watch Selena dance for me.

"From California, Couple 201—Jared Brooks and Viktoria Volkova Brooks."

I choked on my beer. Benny and Karen's son was Benny's latest wife's partner? Vika was Jared's stepmom, for God's sake. It was worse than any daytime soap opera my mother had forced me to watch. These types of incestuous couplings were one of the many reasons I had left this world without looking back many years ago. Not even my love of Selena had made me want to stay.

But here I was, back again.

"From New York, Couple 216—Ricardo Mancini and Elizabeth Young," the announcer said, and then called three more couples to the floor.

"Ladies and gentlemen, let's put those hands together for our Closed Professional International Latin Championship Finalists. Congratulations, competitors. And places for your first dance. The Cha-Cha-Cha. Music, please."

The beat of a cha-cha song filled the room, and Selena brightened. She swirled her hips, flashing her thighs. Dima's jaw went firm; his back straightened like a pole. He gave her a fierce, animalistic look, grabbed her hand, and glided into their routine.

Selena started with a simple cha-cha lock, into fan, as she flirted with the audience. She embraced Dima and draped her arms around his neck, then ran her hands slowly up and down his chest as she did lightning-fast swivels. Dima threw her down into a deep split while caressing her legs.

I had been away from ballroom for so many years, but I could still appreciate how sharp and connected Dima and Selena were. Every inch of their bodies, every step of their feet, every flick of their toes, and every arm movement were perfectly in sync.

Dima pushed Selena into another deep split and then lifted her up to his lips. My own breathing got shallow, quick. She was so alive, on fire, in her element. Maybe she had been right many years ago, choosing dancing over me. Watching her out there, seducing the judges, dancing as if on air—it was clear she belonged on the dance floor.

I was glad I left the lights behind. Joining the Marines was the best choice I had ever made. I didn't want this life, the lifestyle of the famous.

And she'd made it clear she didn't want *mine.*

I studied Selena's face, looking for where the performance stopped, and the real feelings for Dima began. When the song was over, she pushed Dima's face away. But maybe that was just part of the choreography.

I clenched my fist—why did I even care whether Selena and Dima were in a relationship or if their affection was just an act for the cameras?

Seeing Selena compete took my thoughts back to my childhood. My parents were ballroom champions, and I had grown up on the competition circuit. They had forced me to dance, and I had never really enjoyed it. As a kid, it was exciting, traveling around the world like vagabonds. But deep down, I'd always wanted something stable. The kind of life I had imagined the other kids had. Boring, predictable. Normal. Play little league, join Boy Scouts, try out for the football team.

When the kids at school discovered that, instead of spending my free time playing video games and throwing eggs at houses, I was dancing, that was when I'd learned what it was to be a target.

Fag. Sissy. Girl. The taunts had never let up. But I'd been willing to endure the teasing.

For Selena.

After she left me, I'd turned all my focus to the Corps. I became a different man. And that man had vowed never to step on the dance floor again.

On the other hand, that man now had a plan. One season of this show and I'd get the money I needed to fulfill a promise to my best friend—a man who saved my life. It seemed like a small sacrifice.

"The Cha-Cha-Cha. Thank you, competitors."

Dima presented Selena to the audience and judges. The crowd exploded.

"Who's your favorite couple out there, ladies and gentlemen?"

"Couple 187!" someone yelled.

I couldn't resist. I whistled. "Selena!"

"And places for your next dance. Ladies and gentlemen, samba, please."

It had only begun, but Selena was on fire.

***

AN HOUR LATER, all the competitors were lined up in the on-deck area. They'd run through the samba, rumba, paso doble, and jive.

"And the results of the Closed Professional International Latin Dancesport Championship are as follows: Ladies and gentlemen, our runners-up. Placing second in cha-cha, third in samba, second in rumba, second in paso doble, and second in jive—from California, couple 201, Jared Brooks and Viktoria Volkova Brooks."

Jared kissed his stepmother on the cheek, and she giggled. Thank god when my own father had remarried, his new wife wasn't as young and sexy as Vika.

"And ladies and gentlemen, placing first in all dances, your Closed Professional United States International Latin Champions—from California, couple 187, Dmitri Volkov and Selena Martinez."

Selena jumped up and down and kissed Dima on the lips.

An ache twisted in my stomach.

And it wasn't just jealousy. Dima had been our coach when we were kids. He was ten years older than us, which didn't seem like a big deal now that we were in our late twenties but had been a big deal when we were in our tweens. I idolized that motherfucker.

Then he stole my girl.

Spinning four times, they bowed and thanked the crowd. Selena took her place for the event photo. The competition organizer handed her a dozen red roses and their check for the prize.

The night winded down quickly as the spectators milled around the ballroom, saying their goodbyes. The judges vacated their posts. Reporters wandered the room, searching for any available dancers.

I made my way over to the floor.

Wrapping herself in a robe, Selena withdrew from the crowd, Benny following her.

I gazed at Selena and finished my beer. Dima posed for pictures, which was fine by me. I didn't know what I would say to Dima when we finally met again.

I would probably deck him.

Breathe, Bret.

"Congrats, Sel. I'm glad I came to watch."

Selena beamed, still short of breath. "Thanks, Bret." She leaned forward, planting a light kiss on my cheek.

She was sweaty, and her hair was wild. I grinned, looking down, not wanting her to see my face. I'd always liked her like this.

Benny pushed in between us. "Well, I hate to cut this rip-snorter of a party short, but we've just confirmed your assignments. Your celebrity partners want to meet tomorrow. Sorry for the short notice, but this show business thing is highly unpredictable, isn't it?" He opened his jacket and handed some papers to Selena and me.

"San Francisco?" Selena asked, looking up at me.

"Marin, actually. You and Bret are paired with a bloke and his Sheila. I can't tell you their names, but they're icons."

Marin, of course. Benny was sending us to our hometown, where we'd fallen in love so many years ago.

Selena shook her head. "We start tomorrow? I only packed for the competition."

"Sorry, luv. We just got word that they have to start training early because they both have a charity commitment and need to take the following week off when you were supposed to start. They're expecting you both tomorrow evening."

Selena stood there, blotting her head with a towel, the self-tanner staining the fabric. "But there's no flight assignments, just an address. What time is our flight?"

Benny gave a big grin, his gray eyebrow inching up like a worm. Fuck, I knew that look from years ago.

"Well, Selena. That's a great question. You'll be gobsmacked. Bret, Selena, please step outside."

I took a deep breath. I was used to Benny's games but didn't have a clue what he was planning.

Benny signaled to the film crew and led us outside of the hotel.

The etched glass doors separated. A lifted, shiny silver Ford truck stood there in all its glory. It had all the bells and whistles, a huge grill, custom rims, and bright, brilliant headlights.

Benny tossed me the keys. "Bret, m'boy. This is your new truck! Courtesy of Ford. They've donated it to you as a welcome gift for our American Hero!"

My jaw dropped. "Are you messing with me?"

"Nup." Benny opened the truck's door.

I stood there in awe of the truck. I didn't deserve this and definitely didn't want to owe anyone anything. The only reason I agreed to go on this show was to raise money for Pierce's family—not to be showered with gifts that I hadn't earned.

This was unreal. What price would I have to pay for this gift? This Ford Raptor was my dream truck. It had to be worth at least eighty thousand dollars.

More than I made in an entire year. More than I would make on this show.

My stomach ached. How could they just throw money at me? I wouldn't—couldn't—accept this "gift" when my men struggled to make ends meet while risking their lives.

The video camera was just inches from his face.

"It's very generous, Benny, but I can't accept this. It's too expensive. My truck is perfectly fine." My ten-year-old basic-model GMC Sierra needed new brake pads and a fresh coat of paint, but it was paid off and still ran.

Benny signaled the cameras to shut off. "Okay, so the deal is, Ford is sponsoring the show and giving you the truck. In exchange, we're giving them free advertising."

"Out of the question. I won't take it."

Selena butted in. "Bret, take the truck. You don't really have a choice. Ford is one of our sponsors."

My face warmed. I wouldn't be backed into a corner. "I refuse."

Benny put his arm around me. "Mate, you can always sell the ute. We can even do an auction after the season for charity. But you have to ride in it."

"If I have no choice..." My voice trailed off—how would they manipulate me next?

"Attaboy. There's one more thing. They want to film you both traveling in the truck."

"Us both? What does this have to do with Selena?"

"Well, no one knows you yet. Selena's our star! It's just one road trip. For your dead mate." Benny winked at Selena.

Was she in on this bullshit? So now they were going to throw Pierce in my face every time I didn't do what they asked?

"Fuck you, man. And this truck."

I threw the keys on the ground and walked away.

Selena came racing after me.

"Don't, Selena. Just don't. This was a mistake."

She reached for my hand, and I pulled it away.

"No, Bret, wait. You know Benny. He didn't mean anything by that. This is just how the show works. Reality is real, you know?"

Yup, I knew.

I exhaled. I knew I couldn't quit. It was too late to go back. I'd signed the contract knowing full well what Benny was capable of.

I turned and walked back to Benny.

"Sorry, Bret."

I didn't have to accept his apology. I just wanted to get this over with. "So, what's the plan? Any other surprises?"

"There's a camera in the back of the truck that will record your trip. You need to leave tonight."

"Tonight? I have to stop in Los Angeles to get my clothes." Selena bit her lip.

"You two can work out the details. Have a great night." Benny gave me a final handshake, kissed Selena, and sauntered back inside the hotel.

I turned to Selena, whose gown was glowing in the moonlight. "Well, I guess we're leaving tonight."

"I can't believe we have to drive there." Her brow was furrowed like it was the craziest thing ever.

My own forehead crinkled with amusement. "Why?"

"Well...because." She placed her hands on her hips. "I mean, no one drives. They arrange first-class seats, and then a limo picks us up."

"Well, maybe a nice, peaceful drive isn't *your* thing, but it's mine. Especially in this truck. I don't need a plane ticket, and I sure as hell don't need first class."

A thinly painted eyebrow rose while her eyes narrowed. "You're saying I'm high-maintenance?"

Yup, exactly.

I laughed, holding my hands up in protest. "Hey, I never said that did I? I haven't seen you in ten years.

But from what I've read in the magazines...yeah. I'd say you seem like a diva."

She pouted, but her eyes twinkled. "Okay, fine. I can handle a road trip. As long as we can stop tonight at my place so I can get my stuff. And, of course, my bags from the hotel."

"Fine. But only if you don't try filling up the back of my truck with all your fancy luggage."

Selena's gaze hovered to the left, and I saw Dima walk by the lobby with a group of girls. Her eyes darkened, and she whipped her head back with a shrug and a tiny smile. "I'll have the bellman bring it all down, and you'll see for yourself."

"Never mind the bellman. Just give me your room number, and I'll go get it."

Selena's mouth opened, but she didn't answer me.

"What, Selena? Are you on some secret celebrity floor? Do I need a special key?"

"No. It's not that. Are you sure you don't want me to call the bellman?"

I frowned. "Why do I need some other guy to grab stuff I can carry myself?"

Selena lit up and smiled. "I know. It's just...never mind. It's room 632."

I fondled my new keys. "I need to run home and pack. I'll meet you at your hotel room in two hours."

I walked Selena back to the hotel and watched as she went into the elevator. She waved goodbye.

I left the hotel, climbed into my truck, and turned the stereo on. Caressing the leather steering wheel, I flicked on the headlights, roared the engine.

I would enjoy this gift for the season and could sell it for my buddy's family.

But that was the easy part.

I had no desire to spend eight hours holed up in a steel box with the woman who broke my heart.

Bret would be knocking on my door any second. I tossed my clothes into my suitcase. The drive from San Diego to Marin would be nine hours, at least. Would he want to drive all night? Stay at my house in LA? It was already dark out.

Dima was still downstairs, probably flirting with his fans. I debated texting him that I had to leave but decided to write a note instead.

Dima,

Benny said I have to take off to San Francisco tonight to meet my celebrity. I'll call you tomorrow.

Love,

Selena

I chose to omit that Bret would be driving me. It shouldn't matter to Dima. And it wasn't like I had a choice. Crazy as it seemed at first, I was already starting to look forward to it. Some days, I lived at the airport. I was constantly in the air—traveling to train with my celebrities, jetting off to be interviewed on talk shows, hopping on flights for competitions. How exhausting. A nice, slow drive did sound like a welcome change of pace.

Ten years ago, I wouldn't have thought I'd still be competing at age twenty-eight. Back then, ballroom dancing was relegated to the once-yearly televised competition on PBS. There were no weekly celebrity television shows. Though the show gave me the financial security I needed to support my family and my competition career, its demands definitely interfered with the practicing and coaching that we needed to win Blackpool. I had imagined that by this point in my life, I'd have already won my coveted title, be retired, and settled down with a husband and kids. Maybe I'd be running a small dance studio like Bret's mom. But I'd pushed that dream aside for now.

Despite all the insanity with Dima, slipping out of my three-inch suede Latin heels and walking off the dance floor was not an option, not yet. I loved my life and wasn't ready to hang up my ball gown, even though I desperately wanted to start a family. A pulsating samba, a rhythmic cha-cha, a melodic rumba, a confrontational paso doble, a frolicking jive—my body couldn't just stop with it all. Some girls found the mink fur eyelashes, the fake tan, the hair extensions—all of it—heavy. But not me. And when the music died, life was always a little less bright, waiting for the next turn on the sprung hardwood floor.

I had already scrubbed off all of my makeup, stripped off my costume, and washed the glitter out of my hair. Would Bret like the soft terry eggplant-colored designer sweats I usually saved for traveling? No. I folded the suit with care, slipping it into my suitcase. Instead, I reached for a simple white cotton t-shirt and a pair of worn, tight jeans.

I pulled my hair back into a ponytail and perched myself on the edge of my bed but couldn't relax. I grabbed a magazine and flipped through it, all the while staring at the alarm clock. Bret was never late.

A strong rap at the door disrupted the silence. I tossed the magazine on the coffee table and crossed the room to open the door.

Bret stood there, looking stunned. "You didn't even ask who it is. Don't you have stalkers? I could be a sex-crazed fan."

Well, if my sex-crazed fan was as hot as you, he'd have a shot.

I laughed nervously. It was hard not to look at him and remember that he'd been my first love. My first lover. And I'd been his. He'd been a shy, lean teenage boy back then. This Bret standing before me—he was all man. His presence threw me. Made me wonder crazy things. Like what it would be like to nuzzle his neck, fondle his muscles, taste his kisses—those strong hands exploring every inch of my body.

I couldn't let myself go there. We were about to be stuck in a truck for eight hours. I gave a playful roll of my eyes and crossed my arms.

"Relax. I checked in under a pseudonym, and no one else knows my room number. I knew it was you because you're right on time."

Bret slung my duffel bag over his shoulder. "What's your name?"

"What?"

"Your fake name. What is it?"

"If I tell you, I'll have to change it next time."

Bret just stared back at me, clearly not amused.

"Fine, if you must know, it's Brenda Walsh."

He gave me a blank look.

I shot him a skeptical glare. "Oh, come on. *Beverly—*"

"*Hills 90210*, I know. I remember losing weeks of my life watching those garbage reruns, over and over, at every dance competition."

"Well, that's the only American show some of those countries would play. Besides, you got a kick out of the ridiculous dubbed voices. The Spanish Dylan was hilarious."

"Okay, Brenda. Let's get a move on. It's late." Bret stared at Dima's bags in the room. Ugh, now he knew we had shared a room. At least there were two queen beds in it.

I picked up my purse and cooler and followed Bret out the door.

When we arrived downstairs, I focused on the new truck. I'd always liked Dima's flashy Fanta orange Lamborghini, but there was something about this big silver truck that seemed more exciting, more masculine, and less pretentious. Bret tossed my luggage into the bed.

"Um...I thought you were only kidding about putting my things in the back of your truck."

"No, princess, I wasn't. Otherwise, there would be no room for Banjo."

The valet handed Bret his keys and a leash. Attached to the latter was a tan, smooshy-faced dog, around thirty pounds, with a goofy smile. Bret slapped a five-dollar bill in the valet's hand.

"You're bringing . . . your dog? I'm not sure the hotel up there will allow it. What is he, anyway?"

Banjo sniffed me and slobbered all over my jeans. "He's a pug/lab mix. Got him at the base shelter. Great dog. Anyway, I'm not staying in the hotel. Get in, Sel. I'll put a tarp over your bags, so they don't get too many dead bugs."

Gross. The thought of slimy insects smashed over my luggage made me ill. But I wasn't going to make a big deal out of it because I didn't want to endure Bret's teasing.

He helped me into the truck and hoisted Banjo in next to me, and the mutt scampered to the backseat. The fresh scent of new leather tickled my nose. I stole a glance at Banjo, now making himself comfortable by turning in circles on the seat until plopping down. Where would they be staying, if not at the hotel? For all I knew, Bret could have a girlfriend in Marin.

Bret climbed into the front seat, and we were off.

"Are you hungry? We can stop at In-N-Out."

Memories of a fifteen-year-old Bret egging me on to cram the rest of my Double Double Burger Animal Style in my mouth hovered in my mind. Before In-N-Outs were all over California, we once drove two hours away to find Bret's favorite burger. Winning a competition meant a greasy reward we'd never be allowed to eat during training.

Back then, I could eat anything and not gain an ounce.

I pointed at the cooler resting between my feet. "I have my dinner packed."

"I don't even want to ask. Cooler?"

"Uhm yeah. My nutritionist has a chef prepare my meals for me. It's vegan and gluten-free. But super yummy." I reached between my knees, pried the lid open, and pulled out a clear plastic container. "It's this amazing quinoa grilled vegetable salad with lentils and lemon-basil vinaigrette. Wanna try?"

Bret turned his nose up. "I'll pass. Thanks."

He pulled into the drive-through and ordered a few burgers. When he received his food, he unwrapped a plain hamburger and tossed it to Banjo.

Back on the road, we were both silent. The music coming out of the car speakers grew louder, now that Bret had turned up the volume. Eddie Vedder's deep voice belted the song "Black."

Sitting next to Bret was surreal, especially without the buffer of mindless banter to keep my awkwardness from settling over us. He was right there, inches away from me. Years ago, I might've placed my hand on his thigh. Now, Bret stared ahead, navigating the road with a determined expression on his face. Maybe that precise focus was something he'd developed overseas, driving a tank through dusty streets bordered by dilapidated homes. Or perhaps that was just some image I'd picked up from a movie somewhere. I knew nothing of what he'd experienced in Iraq. I wanted to ask about his life. But none of my questions seemed the right one to lead with.

Banjo had finished his burger and was rolling around in the backseat, tan hairs shedding everywhere. I picked at my healthy salad. The tiny grains tumbled off the fork, and I pouted, almost wishing my hands were clutched around a foil-wrapped Double Double instead.

There would never be a perfect moment, so I reached over and lowered the music. "So, Benny mentioned to me about your friend. What happened?"

He sighed. "My buddy, Landon Pierce, was killed in Iraq. He had volunteered to go on a patrol, a patrol that I had been scheduled for, and his Humvee was hit with an IED."

I gasped. "Oh, Bret, that's awful! I'm so sorry."

"Yeah, it sucks. It should've been me."

"Don't say that."

"It's true. He had a wife and two young kids. When Benny wrote, I figured the show would be an easy way to make a bunch of money in a few months. Then I can help Pierce's family out."

A few months? I had assumed there was a chance he would become a regular dancer. That he'd be around for the next few years. At least. "Why only one season? It's a great lifestyle—you only have to work for fifteen weeks twice a year. Dima and I stay on the show so we can afford to compete. We want to win Blackpool within the next two years." I paused, realizing that Bret probably didn't want to hear about my competition plans. "You can raise money for other Marines—if you like it. You should stay on the show."

"No, I can't. This is a one-shot deal for me. I had to get special permission from the Marine Corps. I'm still under orders for two more years. After that, I'll have twelve years in—I can retire at twenty, so I'll just reenlist for eight more."

I lowered my head. "But I'm sure if you wanted to, they could make an exception."

Bret shook his head. "That's not how it works. The military doesn't make exceptions. And I don't want to.

I'm just doing this for Pierce. Otherwise, there's no point."

My voice increased a notch as I tried to hide my anger. "It's hardly pointless. We do good stuff, too. Charity work, fundraisers, that sort of thing. Dima and I even started this program where we teach underprivileged kids how to dance. It's awesome. I've met with sick children and wounded warriors. It's not all tanning salons and talk shows."

Bret laughed. "The whole thing is ridiculous. 'Stars.' How is starring in your own sex tape 'star' material? Or popping out a hundred kids? My buddy died defending the freedom of these buffoons so they could make assholes out of themselves on camera. These reality stars are pathetic. I'd rather live my life than watch people live theirs."

This show, *my life*, was clearly nothing more than a joke to Bret. "We've also trained Olympic athletes and Grammy winners. And I'm a reality star—so are you saying I'm pathetic?" My body heated up. "You trash the show but want to use it for money. Where's your integrity?"

"All the money I make will go back to helping my buddy's family. So, yeah, I know I'm doing the right thing. What do you spend *your* money on? How much is that obnoxious ring on your finger?"

I stared at my 3.7-carat pink diamond ring that Dima had given me when we got engaged six years ago. I now wore it on my right hand instead of my left. But then again, Ukrainians wore their engagement rings on their right hands. Ugh, I was sure Bret thought Dima and I were together.

"Dima got it free from a jeweler who wanted his rings seen on the red carpet. It's *not* an engagement ring. I mean, it was, but we aren't engaged. We aren't even dating right now. It's just a gift." When the words left my mouth, I realized that Bret must think I was awful. I took a nervous sip from my water bottle.

Bret scowled at me. "Whatever you say, Selena. Dima makes hundreds of thousands of dollars a year, and he can't even buy you a ring himself? Hell, I was making five hundred a week at Best Buy and saved up for months to buy you a ring. Not that you appreciated it. The fact that his ring doesn't even mean anything to you makes it worse."

My cheeks warmed. "I didn't say it didn't mean anything to me."

"What's the point of a huge diamond ring if you have no intention of ever getting married? Oh, I forgot—you don't want that simple, I think you once said *boring*, life. But it's cool. I'm sure we'd be divorced by now."

My throat burned. "It wasn't easy for me, either. I loved you, but I was only eighteen, Bret. It was heartbreaking." I blinked back tears, remembering what I'd given up. I considered coming clean and revealing the real reason I had ended it with Bret but didn't have the courage. "I wasn't about to give up my dreams and become a teenage housewife. And I needed to keep dancing to support my family. What would I do on some base in the middle of nowhere while you were fighting wars nine months out of the year? It would've never worked. We were too young. If you wanted to settle down so badly, why aren't you married?"

He looked away from me. "I never met the right woman."

Ouch.

"It's fine. I don't want to get married. Not until I get out of the Corps. I've seen so many divorces, and many of my buddies' wives cheat on them while they're deployed. Then again, many of my men cheat, too. Broken families. Kids never see their dads. Plus, even if I found a great woman, what if I died over there like Pierce did? I'd leave a young widow and my kids without a father."

After all these years, I had hoped Bret had found the family life he'd always craved that I couldn't give him. At least that's what I told myself. To hear that Bret was still alone and had given up hope made me sad.

"You can't live your life like that. What happened to your friend was awful, and I feel so sorry for his family. But that doesn't mean the same fate would await you."

The truck accelerated, nothing drastic, but enough for my water to spill. Banjo jostled in the back.

After a few songs in silence, Bret relaxed into his seat. "So, where do you live? Some gated Beverly Hills mansion? Are there going to be paparazzi waiting for us?"

"Why? Hoping for the cover of *People*?"

"No. I just don't want the Marine Corps to charge me with adultery, with your deep commitment to Dima and all."

"I told you we aren't together, Bret."

"Could've fooled me. Sharing a room, kiss on the floor, huge diamond ring."

Red brake lights blinded me, and I was too tired to focus on anything. "It's not like that, and you know it. You know how ballroom partnerships are. A kiss on the floor means nothing, it's just acting. We book a room together because it's easier to keep all our costumes together. Most times, he ends up crashing at another one of the dancers' rooms anyway. And I already explained to you about the ring."

"Well, don't you have an excuse for everything."

Why was he such a jerk to me?

"Anyway, soldier boy, no, there won't be any paparazzi. It's not like we go around ringing them up and saying, hey, come over, I'll give you a good shot. Jesus, Bret, not everyone on the show is some shallow fame whore. Some of us actually do it because we want to dance."

"First off—Marines aren't soldiers. Marines are Marines or warriors. Army has soldiers."

I laughed. Bret was so uptight. "Sorry, Marine."

I gave him the address, and Bret plugged it into his navigation system. My gaze zeroed in on his large hands, bulging veins, and confident hold on the steering wheel. A fleeting thought entered my sleepy mind, blowing past my consciousness and leaving a trail of even more questions, like what it might be like to feel those hands touching my bare skin.

Warmth climbed up my neck, and I shook the thought away, scolding myself. As much as I was attracted to his fantastic body, masculine scent, and deep voice, I had to remind herself that Bret's reappearance into my life would only be brief.

Sure, I could have a fling with him, but I knew I would end up getting hurt when he left again.

Besides, all he did was give me a hard time about my choices. He infuriated me. Drove me completely crazy.

And if I allowed myself to get used to him being around, then I'd have to learn to live without him.

Again.

I maneuvered my brand-new truck up the winding Hollywood Hills. Towering trees framed the street, and it was difficult to focus on the road. Being this close to Selena unnerved me. Despite the fact that she drove me absolutely crazy with her spoiled and selfish outlook on the world, she looked and smelled incredible. I tried to keep my mind on the road and not on thinking about kissing her neck, tasting her lips, and caressing her body.

"It's the next driveway. Just enter Code 0114 in the keypad."

I eyed Selena. January fourteenth was the anniversary of the day Selena and I won Nationals.

Selena seemed to understand my questioning look. "Don't get all weird on me. It was just the first major competition I—I mean we—ever won. It doesn't mean anything."

"Sure, it doesn't."

I turned into the driveway and pressed the numbers into the black alarm pad. A huge gate opened, and I drove to the front of Selena's house. It was less extravagant than I had expected, just an old Spanish-style bungalow with talavera tiles framing the entrance, not some sprawling Hollywood mansion.

Selena took the keys out of her purse and opened the door. "It's super late, and I'm beat. Are you sure you don't want to crash here tonight? We can leave as early as you want tomorrow morning."

I hoisted Banjo out of the backseat of the truck, attached his leash, and led him to a bush to pee. It was dark, so I couldn't read Selena's face. She had just invited me to spend the night. I wasn't sure I could sleep in the same house as her. "I'm not sure if that's a good idea."

Selena just laughed and turned on the lights. "Relax, Bret. It's really not a big deal. You can use the guesthouse out back."

Guesthouse? I should've known that there was more to her house. It sure made my tiny place off base look like a slum. She'd probably laugh if she saw my small apartment, which was about the size of her living room.

In the main house, there were red tiles on the floor and dark wooden beams on the ceiling. Her yellow-painted walls had pictures of Dima and Selena everywhere: winning competitions, on the television show, on the red carpet. But I was taken aback when I noticed a framed picture of Selena and me winning Nationals. The same picture from the magazine cutout Benny had sent.

"Why do you still have this picture up?"

Selena smiled. "It was my first national win."

I remembered that night well. After we celebrated with Dima, who had coached us, I told Selena I loved her for the first time.

Banjo jumped up on Selena's brown leather sofa and curled into a ball.

"Well, I'm tired too. So just show me the guesthouse, and I'll get out of your hair. We have to leave at zero six hundred tomorrow morning."

Selena laughed. "I'll assume you mean six a.m. But it's okay, Bret. You can relax—we don't have to be there until five in the evening."

"I don't like to be late. Punctuality was never your strong suit if I remember correctly."

Selena walked into the kitchen and opened the refrigerator door. "Do you want a beer? Dima mostly stocks Vodka, but he does have some Russian beer."

"So, Dima fills your fridge, too? What else do you do together? File taxes? You sound married."

"Stop, Bret. I have a place here, and he has one closer to the studio in Glendale. Sometimes he crashes here —in the guesthouse. How about that beer?"

I would've loved a beer to relax and take the edge off the tension in the room. But I didn't trust myself alone with Selena.

Before I could decline, Selena popped off the cap of a bottle and handed it to me.

Why was she being so nice to me? Probably because she broke my heart and felt guilty. If it were any other woman, I would be certain she was flirting.

I studied the label, written in Russian letters. "*Peba?* What's this crap?" I took a swig. It tasted like vinegar. "You don't have a Corona? I guess Dima's taste hasn't changed." But beer is beer. I took another sip and then sat on the sofa to pet Banjo.

"*Peva.* Yeah. It's not the best, but Dimka loves it."

Dimka? Hearing my old coach referred to like that was...well, creepy. Dima had been a twenty-two-year-old man when he'd started teaching us as kids. A ten-year age difference wasn't a big deal now that Selena was a woman in her late twenties, but I couldn't help but be disturbed by the way I thought Dima had groomed her to be his.

Selena took her own bottle and settled in next to me.

I inched my way over to the other end of the sofa and looked around the room. This place was incredible—must be worth at least a million dollars, probably more, hidden up in the hills. This could've been my home, my life, my sofa, my woman, but the fridge would be stocked with craft beers. At the time I gave up dancing, there was little hope for a career besides running a studio and spending all the revenue on competing. Now Selena and Dima were millionaires.

I wasn't jealous; I hated competing and truly loved being a Marine. But I never thought for a second that I would be struggling to make ends meet, with little hope of ever buying a house in San Diego or Marin.

She took a long sip and then sighed. "Bret, I need to get this off my chest. So, I know it was ten years ago, but I just really want to say how sorry I am about what went down. It was the hardest decision—"

Not doing this. "Selena, don't. It's fine. It was forever ago. I don't want to talk about it."

She pursed her lips and looked at me. "Well, I do. There was so much going on and—"

I didn't want to hear her excuses for walking out on me. Plus, for all I knew, she was miked, and this pathetic apology would play out on television. "I said it's cool. Just forget it."

She put her hand casually on my leg.

Heat pooled to my body. I imagined her hand sliding up my thigh.

Nope. She was so fucking hot. I was dying to fuck her, but I just couldn't let myself go there.

I moved her hand off and stood up.

"Thanks for the beer, Sel. I really need to get some sleep." I motioned to Banjo, and the dog jumped down.

She bit her lip, a dejected look on her face. "Oh, sure. I'll show you the casita."

"I'm just gonna grab my bag." I opened the front door and went to my truck. I looked up to the dark blue, starry sky. I hadn't signed up for this emotional drama. The producers were probably strumming up drama, and I wouldn't allow it. There was no way I was going to play into some twisted love triangle. I didn't believe for a second that Selena and Dima weren't still hooking up.

I wanted to jump into this truck and head back down to my place and rip up the dance contract. But I was a man of my word and wouldn't go back on my promise to Pierce.

I was now sure of one thing—being this close to Selena for the next fifteen weeks would require some serious self-control.

A loud rap at my bedroom door roused me from my dreams.

"Sel, we need to get a move on. Are you awake?"

Hearing Bret's voice first thing in the morning was a welcome surprise. "Yeah, sorry. I'll be out in a few minutes."

"I'll make coffee."

Ah. That was sweet. I rolled onto my back and closed my eyes. Last night, I'd dreamt about Bret. Over the years, he'd been the star of many of my dreams. But this dream was different. We were dancing together, after all these years. He lacked Dima's speed and technical skill, but Bret's dancing had something that

Dima's didn't—emotion. *Real* emotion, not the fake, flashy, showy moves Dima and I were known for. Bret had always danced from his heart.

Was that gone? Would he ever fall in love with dancing again? He swears he hated it, but I know he didn't. He used to love it. When he was in love with me.

I crawled out of bed and stepped onto the ice-cold marble tile. A quick shower, and we'd embark on the rest of today's journey.

~

I emerged from my bedroom and poured myself a cup of coffee from a fresh pot that Bret had brewed. My nostrils tingled, and when I took a sip, the warm liquid soothed my throat.

Once I could focus, my eyes fell on Bret, who sat on my sofa reading a book. Banjo lay by his feet. The sight of him, relaxed and comfortable in my house, threw me. Had I made a different choice, this could be the setting of my daily life. Bret making me coffee, reading before he headed to work. Maybe getting the kids ready for school. My gut clenched.

"What are you reading?"

Bret glanced up at me. "Oh, just some war book." He closed the cover. "You ready? We really need to get going."

"Yeah. Let me finish my coffee, and we can bounce. Where are you staying up there?"

"My dad bought a houseboat in Sausalito. He lives with his new wife up in Washington, so he said I can stay there while I train."

"How cool! I've always wanted to live on a houseboat. To have the ocean rock me to sleep. I used to babysit for a family who lived on one."

Bret stood up and took the keys out of his pocket. "It beats staying in a hotel. Hotels remind me of the barracks. Let's get a move on."

I made my way to the sink to rinse my coffee cup. An engine hummed outside the window. That was weird —the gardeners weren't supposed to come until Tuesday.

I peeked out the kitchen window. A bright yellow taxi stood out front.

The front door opened. "Selenichka!"

Banjo barked and scampered out of the kitchen.

I dropped my coffee mug. The ceramic shattered on the floor, and Bret and I stared at the little shards.

Nothing had happened between Bret and me last night, but even so, I felt uncomfortable with Dima finding Bret here.

Because Dima was the reason I broke up with Bret.

Dima walked into the kitchen. His mouth opened when he saw Bret crouched on the floor with me, gathering the pieces of the mug.

"What's going on here? I call and text to you all the night. Benny gave me name of hotel, and they said that you did not go to there."

Uh-oh. I had seen the texts, and I'd intended to text him back, but I just had been so exhausted.

I could see Bret staring at the house key Dima was holding. Another item that made it look like Dima and I were still together. Who could blame Bret for thinking that?

I grabbed the dustpan under the sink. "Dimka, I'm sorry. It was just so late—"

Bret reached out his hand to Dima. "Hey, Dima. Sorry about that, it's my fault. We were supposed to drive all night, but I was tired, so Selena said I could stay in the guesthouse. You guys danced great last night. Congrats."

I knew that Dima would never settle for a handshake. He probably still saw Bret as his little disciple. He embraced his old student. "Bret, great to see you, my friend! I thought you go to the war?"

I breathed a sigh of relief as I swept up the ceramic shards. Dima stood with his shoulders relaxed and his feet wide apart. Did he feel a pang of jealousy knowing that Bret spent the night in my house? Even though Dima and I weren't together, deep down, I always thought that Dima figured I would take him back at any time. But that wasn't true, though I had figured that in some ways, Dima was my only option.

Bret pulled back from the hug. "I did go to war. But I'm back now. Just doing a season to raise money for my friend's family. He was killed in Iraq."

Dima seemed impressed by Bret's selflessness. He sat at the table and poured himself a cup of coffee. "This friend of yours. How much money does his family need? I could give to you now. Selena and me, we would love to help."

There Dima went again—flaunting his money around. Maybe he thought he could buy Bret off, so he wouldn't have to worry about me getting close to him.

Bret shook his head. "Thanks, Dima, I really appreciate your offer, but I got this. And I'd love to stay and catch up, but we really need to get on the road."

"Sure, it is no problem." Dima eyed me.

"Sel, I'm gonna take Banjo outside. We have to leave in five minutes. Dima, it was great seeing you again." Bret headed toward the front door, and I heard it shut.

"Sorry, Dima. Bret won this truck, and Benny said—"

Dima cut me off. "I know. Benny told to me everything. I don't have to start with my partner until two more weeks. I come with you before I go."

Why did he want to join me in San Francisco? We never visited each other when we were training our celebrities. Not since we had been together romantically. "You don't have to."

"Of course, I do not. But I want to go to there. We need to train for Blackpool. It is in four months. And

San Francisco is our home. Where we met, where we fell in love. We were supposed to get married there."

Dima never brought up our broken engagement. I couldn't believe he was doing this. Right now. When Bret was outside.

"Whatever, Dimka. You called off the engagement. You needed your space before we settled down and got married, remember? And you haven't been missing me when you have been with all your women."

Breathe, Selena, breathe.

"Anyway, Bret's nervous enough. Having you around would hurt his chances on the show. You owe him that, don't you think?"

Dima stayed silent. We had an unspoken promise never to talk about what had led me to finally make the decision to leave Bret.

Honestly, I didn't have a choice.

"I really have to go. I'll call you when I get there."

"*Ya tebya loobloo.*"

I paused. "I love you, too." We always said those words to each other. And I did love Dima. But I'd long given up any hope that we could have a normal relationship. Watching him over the years, dating the starlets on the show, had forced me to push my feelings aside.

I left the table, went to my bedroom, and grabbed my rolling suitcase. Dima was acting strangely, like he could read my mind. Being near Bret made me yearn for the pure love that I'd once shared with him. I had convinced myself that what Bret and I had shared was only possible for a young, first-time love.

I walked out the front door. Bret hopped out of his truck and took my bags. "Everything alright?"

"Yes. I'm great. Let's go."

Bret helped me into the truck. I settled into the crackly leather of the front seat, looking forward to our journey ahead.

BRET

Once we finally hit the road, I still couldn't relax. I hated uncertainty. In the Marine Corps, my life was regimented. I knew what time I had to wake up every morning, what time I was supposed to work out, when each meal would be, and exactly what was planned for work. As I drove up the I-5 freeway, my eyes dulled by the endless views of dirt and cow pastures, I had no idea how this day, or any after it, would unfold. And I hated it.

Selena looked out the window. Surprisingly, she had been mostly silent for the past three hours of the trip.

"So, what normally happens on the first day? We just have to meet them today, right? No dancing?"

Selena turned to me, smiling. "Yeah, pretty much. The cameramen are there when you meet your stars. But sometimes it takes a few shots before they get it right, so you have to keep looking surprised every time they open the door. It isn't too bad."

Might not be too bad for Selena—she had always been good at hiding her feelings. I was no actor, though, and wasn't looking forward to faking it for the cameras. "Well, I hope they get my shot on the first try."

"You'll be fine. I wonder who our celebrities are? Any ideas?"

I couldn't care less who my partner was. I just wanted to get through this season without embarrassing myself, my friend's family, and the Corps. "Hell if I know, Sel. I don't follow all that celebrity stuff. Probably just some washed-up stars like the usual losers who go on this show."

"You are so judgmental." Selena scowled at me. "I'm excited. Only cool, reclusive celebrities live in Marin. I'm sure they're awesome."

"I'm sure they are just as spoiled as the Los Angeles celebrities. I've met some overseas through the USO.

Some turned into jerks the second the cameras weren't on them."

"That's too bad. But by living up here, they're probably more down-to-earth. Don't you think?"

I decided to stop talking. I had almost forgotten that there was a camera in the back of this truck recording our every word. In five weeks, nineteen million people would be watching Selena and I bicker in my truck.

~

Three hours later, we finally arrived in Marin. It was in the afternoon, and we had to meet our celebrities at five. I exited on Tiburon Boulevard and headed to the Tiburon Lodge, where we were set to meet our hair and makeup staff.

Driving down the winding road, I took in the beauty of the San Francisco Bay. I loved it here—the green grass and walking trails of Blackie's Pasture, the view of the towering Golden Gate Bridge. At least I would be spending a few months in this paradise, and since I had used all of my vacation time for the show, I figured I'd better enjoy it. Ray was right—this definitely beat dodging land mines in Iraq.

We pulled up to the hotel, and I parked in the lot. I didn't want a valet to touch my truck.

"Sel, we have two hours before we have to meet production. I'm gonna take Banjo on a walk through Blackie's Pasture before I have to drop him at my dad's houseboat." I looked up, and her eyes seemed hopeful. I really wanted to be alone, but I didn't want to strand Selena. "Do you want to come with us or stay here?"

Her face brightened. "I'd love to take a walk. I'll just change into my running shoes."

She walked around to the bed of the truck, and I pulled her luggage down. I grabbed a tennis ball, some treats, and doggie bags.

She rummaged through her bag, found her shoes, and tossed her flip-flops back in. I placed her bag in the backseat of the truck. "Let's go."

We crossed the street and walked toward the path. I loved the salty smell of the bay. I really needed this break from the Marine Corps, even if I was still working.

"It's so nice," Selena said. "In Los Angeles, there's so much smog, and it's never clear. I miss it here. Do you ever want to move back?"

"It's beautiful, but I'll never be able to afford it. And it's too liberal for my taste. Anyway, there are more jobs for former military down in San Diego. You?"

Selena sighed. "I'd love to, but Dima and I own a studio in LA. But I think Marin would be a great place to settle down and raise kids."

We came across the off-leash dog park. I released Banjo, who scampered with a Goldendoodle and a Sheltie.

"When's that going to happen? Settling down, I mean. Are you dating anyone?"

She turned away from me and looked across the bay. "No. I have no time with the show and competing." Her voice dropped. "And I don't ever meet anyone who understands my lifestyle."

I knew it wasn't my place to say anything, but I couldn't resist. "It's your life. Do whatever makes you happy. But a title from Blackpool isn't going to keep you warm at night or take care of you when you're sick."

Selena was still turned away from me, and I couldn't see her face. I knew I had upset her. She'd been back in my life for two days, and that picture-perfect world of hers started to look chipped and cracked the closer I got to it.

"I need to get back to the hotel to get ready," she said, her voice meek. "I'll just start walking back. You and Banjo enjoy the view."

"You sure? I can walk you back." I knew I'd struck a chord.

"Yeah, I'm fine. I might take a nap before hair and makeup. I'll see you later."

"Okay. I'll see you in front of your hotel at four forty-five."

She waved as if to acknowledge me but spoke no words as she walked away.

I threw the tennis ball, and Banjo ran to retrieve it. I didn't feel sorry for Selena; she'd chosen her life just as I'd chosen mine. When we were younger, I had always imagined we would have a life together—kids, dogs, a house, the whole picture. But neither of our lives had worked out that way.

Banjo brought the ball back to me and dropped the chewed-up toy on my feet. After twenty minutes of playing, I headed back to my truck and drove to my father's houseboat.

I was glad to finally be alone. I stepped onto the rickety wood of the dock and walked down the row of houseboats. Each one was unique: one had a Chinese awning; another had brightly colored planter boxes. I was thankful that my dad had purchased this place, and I wouldn't have to spend the next fifteen weeks in a hotel room next to Selena.

I opened the door and scanned the room. It was simple and masculine. My father had been in the Navy before his own dance competition days and had decorated the place with a nautical theme. When I'd joined the Marines instead of the Navy, my dad had been furious. I would always tease my dad that the U.S. Marine Corps is part of the Navy—the men's department.

Banjo ran around the houseboat, checking out his new space. He jumped on me and gave him a slobbery kiss.

"Hey, buddy!" I rubbed Banjo's ears. Lately, Banjo was the only one who kissed me. It had been a long time since I'd connected with anyone. I wasn't a monk; I'd found comfort over the years with some women. But I had always been upfront about not wanting a relationship and would extricate myself from the situation if I became too involved.

I put a leash on Banjo and decided to go for a walk to get a bite to eat.

A lady with gray-streaked hair waved to me. "Hello, I'm Gerta. I live in the next boat. You must be George's boy. He always talks so highly of his hero son."

There was that word again. Hero. "Hi. Yes, ma'am, I'm Bret. Nice to meet you. And this fellow here is Banjo."

Her long, flowy dress shifted in the wind. "Your father said that you were up here filming some television show? I don't have a television, so I don't keep up with all that Hollywood nonsense."

At least I'd met someone else who had better things to do with her time than care about this show. "Yeah. I'm one of the new professional dancers on this season of *Dancing Under the Stars.*"

Gerta's eyebrows perked up. "Whom are you dancing with up here?"

I had no idea, but even if I did, I wasn't supposed to tell anyone my celebrity partner until the big media blitz. But Gerta seemed harmless enough; she didn't even own a television.

"I honestly don't know yet, ma'am. But I'll let you know when I find out."

Gerta's blue eyes sparkled. "Where are you heading?"

Normally I would've been annoyed by this stranger interrogating me, but she was probably just being friendly. "To Fish to get some chowder."

"Oh, I love Fish. Would you mind some company? I'm a widow and get lonely eating alone—though Issaquah Dock is the best houseboat community. We're a wonderful group of creative spirits. I'm a sculptor. And we're one of the few docks that's dog friendly. If you would like me to watch him on the days while you train, I'd be honored."

I smiled. That was the nicest offer I'd had in a long time. I hated the thought of leaving Banjo alone. "Banjo would love that. And I'd love for you to join me for a late lunch." I offered Gerta my arm.

Her shoulders wiggled. She took my arm, and Banjo led the way.

I needed a friend up here. Selena couldn't be the only one I knew. I couldn't be around her any more than I had to. In the past twenty-four hours, I had been unable to stop thinking about her. Imagining what it would be like to kiss her, taste her again. But she was completely off-limits. I still wasn't convinced that she and Dima weren't involved. And even if she was single, we had nothing in common besides our childhood bond.

I couldn't allow Selena to make me lose focus of what I'd come here to do. Pierce's family needed that money. No way could I let myself get wrapped up in some childhood love that couldn't and shouldn't ever be recreated.

SELENA

I leaned back in the chair and allowed the makeup artist to put the finishing touches on my mascara. I loved the first day of shooting. The celebrities were usually so excited, especially since the reality of the training they were about to endure hadn't hit them yet.

"There you go, Miss Martinez. Beautiful. The purple eyeliner brings out the golden flecks in your eyes."

I blinked and stared in the mirror. My eyes did seem brighter than normal, despite the fact that I was exhausted. For the road trip, I had rocked a natural makeup look even though I would've preferred to scrub my face clean. But I had been aware of the cameras in the backseat. "Thank you, Heather."

I had already changed into my greeting outfit. Nothing fancy; the producers wanted to make it seem as if it was a casual meet and greet. I wore a peach-colored sweatsuit paired with Louboutin high heels and some gold hoop earrings. I left my chair, grabbed my purse, and hurried out to Bret's truck for our journey up the hill to our celebrities.

As I approached the truck, Bret shifted on his feet. He hadn't changed his clothes at all. I guessed that wardrobe wanted to portray him as a rough-and-tough Marine to keep him distinct from the other dancers.

Didn't matter, though. He was still the sexiest man. He looked like he could be an action hero.

Upon closer inspection, I learned the truth. So much for the rough-and-tough theory; he'd been doused with foundation and gel. He must've been livid.

"Hey, gorgeous."

Gorgeous? That was the nicest thing he had said to me since we had met again. Maybe we were turning a corner.

"Hello, handsome." I climbed into the truck. "You know, pink is a great color on your lips. Maybe next time we could add some gloss for shine."

"Very funny."

The celebrities' house was only minutes away, up the street. A van followed behind us, carrying camera equipment. We turned into the driveway. As if the gates were expecting us, they opened, and Bret drove through.

"Here we go," Bret sighed.

Then reality kicked in. Christian Louboutin heels *hurt*. I hobbled along the paved driveway in my heels, praying that I didn't face-plant and crash into the camera. Why did it always need to be an *inch* from my face?

"Okay, Bret," the director said. "You need to pretend that you're a huge fan of your celebrity. Act surprised!"

"What if I don't know who she is?"

I rolled my eyes. He was impossible.

The director shook his head. "Well pretend!"

Bret rang the doorbell.

The beveled-wood door opened—and Latin guitar legend Xavier Quintana stood in front of us, his gorgeous television star wife, Robyn, beside him.

I took the lead. "¡*Ay, Dios Mío!* Xavier Quintana? I'm your biggest fan! I love dancing to your music. 'Loteria Queen' is my favorite cha-cha song ever." I didn't even have to pretend—I was thrilled.

Bret reached out and shook Xavier's hand. He turned his attention to Robyn. "Nice to meet you, Robyn. My name is Bret Lord."

"Cut!" the director yelled. He placed his hands on Bret's shoulders. "Bret, this is a television show. Speak a little slower, seem a little more enthusiastic. Maybe give Robyn a hug."

I stifled a laugh. Bret gave me a dirty look.

The door shut, and we made our way back down the staircase.

Bret rang the bell again, and immediately Xavier opened the door.

I once saw on MTV that this guy had some dude whose sole job in life was to hold his boss's umbrella, yet *El Rey* opened his own door? So much for reality.

Xavier wore his own brand *Xavier Tomás* white track-suit with what looked like 4-carat diamond studs in each ear.

I repeated my same enthusiastic intro, and Bret stuck out his hand. "Hi, Robyn. I'm so excited to meet you."

"Cut!" the director shouted. "Okay, let's do it again. Xavier, go back inside." The director grabbed Bret's hand. "Bret, son, I want to hear you scream or shriek. Tell her you're her number one fan."

"I don't scream or shriek. I'm a *man*."

This would be a long night.

I rebalanced my oversized handbag and dance shoes, took a deep breath, and made my way down the stairs. Again. I knew Bret's only hope to get through the shot was for me to project enough cheesiness for both of us.

Take three. Bret rang the bell, and Xavier opened the door.

"Oh my God!" I shrieked as brainlessly as I could. "I can't *believe* I'm dancing with you! I *love* your music!" I leaned into hug Xavier. His breath reeked of tequila.

Xavier's head cocked to the side, and he embraced me. "Thanks, girl," he said, way too loud. "I hear you're the best chica on the show. I need to win this. You game?"

"Hell, yeah—"

"Cut!" The director waved us back. "Selena, that was great. Bret, I need you to at least smile at Robyn. You look like you're at a funeral. One more time, people."

"How long is this gonna take?" Xavier yelled at the director. "I don't have time for amateurs."

I could see a vein in Bret's biceps bulge. He had been right—celebrities in Marin were just as spoiled as they were in Los Angeles.

"Don't worry, Xavier, I'll take care of it."

Xavier slammed the door in the director's face.

The director leaned into Bret. "Bret, this time, just lean in and give Robyn a kiss. You don't have to say anything. C'mon, people, let's try to get this before I die of old age. Hustle, hustle!"

I stumbled back down the driveway for take number four, nearly killing myself twice. Stupid beautiful shoes.

We walked up the stairs, cameras trailing behind us.

Four takes later, the introduction was finally filmed. Bret and I stood in the entryway.

Robyn moved toward Bret, her eyes tracing his body. My stomach clenched. Robyn looked stunning, even better in person. She wore her hair in a natural, short afro. The actress was famous for playing a sexy cougar on her hit daytime soap opera. The tabloids always printed rumors of her affairs with her costars.

Would Robyn turn her charms on Bret? Or maybe the tabloids were just harassing Robyn the same way they harassed Dima and me.

"Bret, are you new to the show? I've never seen you."

Bret nodded his head. "Yes, ma'am. This is my first and only season. I used to be a competitive ballroom dancer—Selena was actually my partner. We won the U.S. Championship as teens. I'm currently a Staff Sergeant in the United States Marine Corps. I'm just doing one season to raise money for my buddy's family. He was killed in Iraq. But I assure you, I know how to dance and will work very hard to get us into the finals."

Xavier put his arm around Bret. "A Marine, huh? I tried to enlist for 'Nam but I couldn't because I suffered from tuberculosis. Thank you for your service."

Robyn's lips parted and formed into a slow smile. "What an amazing story, Bret. I'm honored to be your first and only celebrity partner." She brushed against him. "Please, why don't both of you come in, and we can get to know each other."

The camera zoomed in on Bret's face. For a second, I thought he would push it away, but he clenched his teeth and walked into the home.

A strong scent of sage filled the air. We stepped into the sunken living room, with glass walls and French doors leading to the deck.

Robyn lingered in the hallway. "Can I offer you a drink? Wine, beer, iced tea, tequila, mojito?"

"No, thank you, ma'am."

"Please, Bret, call me Robyn."

I held back a laugh—Bret was so cute, all polite and nervous. "I'll take water."

Robyn went to the kitchen.

Though Xavier must've been at least sixty years old, I found him very attractive. His long dark curls hung on his face, covering his soulful eyes. My mother was a huge Quintana fan. Actually, my first concert had been to see him when I was a child. The man played a guitar as if he were seducing a woman. With his rhythm and my talent, we were a shoo-in to make the finals.

Robyn reappeared with a glass of water with a sliver of lime. "Please, sit down."

"Okay—cut!" the director yelled. "We got what we needed. We'll see you all tomorrow for the first dance practice."

Bret relaxed his shoulders. The cameramen packed up and exited the front door. I was so used to the cameras that I had forgotten they were even there.

Bret tapped his feet. I knew that he wanted to spend as little time here as necessary. "Thank you both so much for welcoming us into your home. Both Bret and I are beat—we traveled from Los Angeles this morning. If you wouldn't mind, we'd love to get some sleep so we can start early tomorrow morning."

Xavier stood up. "Of course. We have a studio in the pool house, so we can both train down there. I don't wake up too early. Can we start around eleven?"

"Sure, that sounds great." I gulped down my water and gave Xavier a hug and Robyn a kiss on the cheek. "I'm so excited about the season. I hope we all make it to the finals."

Robyn clutched my hand. "We will. Have a great night. Nice to meet you."

Bret waved to Robyn and Xavier and headed toward the door. He took the stairs two at a time, reaching the bottom at a jog.

Once safely inside the truck, I turned to Bret. "See, it wasn't that bad. They were nice."

Bret's lip curled. "Sure, they were nice enough. Too bad we got paired with a couple of hippies. Tuberculosis? How convenient. He probably burnt his draft card and then protested the war. True spirit... Man, I can't stand that New Age crap. And what was with that incense smell? They were probably smoking weed. Next thing you know, they'll want us to meditate and go on a vision quest."

That was it. I'd had enough. "You haven't changed a bit, huh? You are so closed-minded. Not everyone has to share your views on life. It's America, Bret. You know, the country that you fight so hard to protect. You're defending our freedom to be individuals, not self-righteous clones." Everything was black or white to Bret. Not a single shade of gray. Or pink. When we were young, I thought I could change him. But clearly this older Bret was even more set in his ways.

I considered myself a freethinker. Open, liberal, honest. The more time I spent with Bret, the more I realized that we were way too different to ever make a relationship work.

"Don't talk to me about freedom," he said. "I've watched my buddies die protecting our country. Of course, everyone has the right to believe in whatever ludicrous ideas they want to. Just like I have the right not to be forced to listen to their crap."

Bret pulled up in front of the hotel and scribbled his number down on a napkin. "Good night, Sel. Call me if you need anything. I'll just be five minutes away. See you tomorrow."

I took the paper and then watched as he drove away. Walking into the lobby, all I wanted was a good night's sleep. Tomorrow, I could focus on dancing, and stop stressing about the life I could've never had with Bret.

$\sim$

The next morning, I sat at Caffe Acri in downtown Tiburon sipping my vanilla latte. The rich roast of the espresso beans was divine, and the strong vanilla syrup didn't have a hint of an aftertaste. If I'd been in LA, I'd have felt guilty that the milk wasn't fat-free, and the syrup contained real sugar. But in Marin, I was at peace, especially since the barista designed cool latte art in the shape of a heart.

Bret would be by any minute to pick me up. I looked out on a ferry docked on the bay. I'd forgiven Bret for his judgments last night and was ready to start fresh. I could open up his mind. Maybe on a day off, Bret and I could ditch practice and take the ferry to San Francisco. When we were kids, we used to watch the skateboarders shred around the Embarcadero. Bret always wanted to jump in and join them, but I wouldn't let him, fearing he'd be injured and unable to dance.

Last time Dima and I came to San Francisco to compete, I was saddened to learn that all the skaters had vanished, banned by the city. The new generation probably had nice skate parks. But my fond memories of seeing the young teens breaking the rules and living on the edge had always been a welcome change from my life back then of nonstop training and competing. Maybe I should've let Bret break the rules, but young me always had been completely focused. My goal had always been to be a ballroom champion—no matter the cost.

My phone blinked with a text from Bret. I looked outside. His truck was stopped in front of the coffee shop.

I gathered my latte and purse and walked outside.

"Hey." I cautiously climbed up onto the seat of the high-lifted truck. I decided to ease into the conversation, hoping Bret had calmed down from the previous night. "Did you have a good night?"

Bret looked more relaxed than he had yesterday. A loose polo shirt wrapped tightly around his bulging biceps. Dima had nice, lean, toned arms, but nothing like Bret's strong muscles.

I turned my head away from him and stared out the window—afraid he would read my mind and know that I was imagining what his pecs and abs must look like underneath his shirt.

"Yes. Just ordered pizza, then watched a Warriors game with Banjo. Perfect night. And my neighbor is watching Banjo today, so he won't be lonely."

"Neighbor? A lady, I presume? One night in town and you already have a new girlfriend," I teased playfully, at the same time praying he hadn't already met someone.

"Yeah. She's a looker. Old enough to be my mother, though I guess that's the 'in thing' these days. Hey, you should get yourself one of those boy-toys that are all the rage."

"A boy toy? I'm twenty-eight. So some eighteen-year-old? No thanks. I want a man."

Bret glared at me. "That's the same age difference of Dima and you. And you dated, didn't you?"

Dammit. Yes. When was I going to tell him why I had actually left him? What had happened that night with Dima and me. Didn't he have the right to know?

But Dima had sworn me to secrecy. And no matter how many times I replayed that night in my head, I couldn't come to peace with it.

"That's different."

"Really, Sel? How so? Because he groomed you?"

The heat shot through me. I wasn't going to get into this with him now.

"That's your opinion. When I'm ready to be in a relationship, I'd like to find someone my age who wants to settle down. One that likes football and drinks craft beers. I'm so sick of watching hockey and drinking vodka."

"Good luck with that, Selena. What kind of man would put up with you dancing with Dima, having your ex run his hands all over your body, you two sharing hotel rooms together?"

"Whatever. Dima and I are just friends."

"Really? Then text him now, 'Let's fuck.'"

I seethed. "You're an asshole, Bret."

"Never said I wasn't. You'll never quit dancing until you win Blackpool—right?"

I clenched my teeth. "Right. But dancing isn't cheating. The emotions aren't real." Winning the Blackpool professional Latin championship had been my goal since I was a little girl. Dima and I had finaled three times, and each year we were closer to winning the title. Even though we'd ended our personal relationship, we still competed together. I had spent ten years training for this goal. What sense would there be in starting over from scratch?

"Well, maybe for you," Bret said. "When we danced together, there was nothing fake about my feelings. Training a celebrity student is one thing. But competing around the world, traveling, sharing hotel rooms with another man, wouldn't be acceptable. Not to me—not to most guys."

We pulled up to the Quintanas' house. I blinked back tears. When the truck stopped, I jumped out and slammed the door.

I jogged up the front stairs. I would focus on training Xavier today. I needed some clarity, and everything would be back to normal. Like it had been before Bret reappeared into my life.

The sunlight from the bay bounced off the mirrors in Robyn and Xavier's ballroom. This room was normally used as their yoga/meditation studio, hence the crimson-colored velvet fabric draped under the ceiling.

"That's it, Robyn. Four and one, two, three, four and one, two, three."

Robyn's hips shimmied across the floor. For her first day, I was impressed. Robyn worked very hard and had an excellent sense of rhythm, not to mention killer legs. I had taught her rumba walks and cha-cha timing.

"Thanks, Bret. This is so much fun." Robyn grabbed her bottle of water and sat on the sofa.

Across the room, Selena trained a struggling Xavier. Unlike Robyn, he was clumsier than I had thought he would be. Selena sure had her work cut out if they wanted to final—or even make it past the first week. I didn't wish to see Selena eliminated, but I had to admit it would be so much easier to focus if she wasn't around.

I gazed at Selena. Robyn put her hand on my shoulder. "So, what's the deal with you two, anyway? Have you kept in touch over the years?"

I had planned a standard answer regarding my relationship with Selena, just in case anyone in the media asked. But I wanted to be honest with Robyn. I turned off my mike, motioned for Robyn to do the same, and then sat next to her.

"We danced together for ten years until we were eighteen. We got engaged, and then I joined the Marines. We were supposed to get married after boot camp. But she left me and decided to dance with Dima. We haven't seen each other since, until a few days ago."

"Well, if you two are soul mates, you'll find your way back to one another. If not in this lifetime, then in the next."

I swallowed and hoped the camera didn't catch my look of unease. I liked Robin and didn't want to disrespect her beliefs, but there was no next lifetime for me. Though I wasn't raised with a faith I became very religious during my first tour in Iraq. I'd attended church every week, and when I'd returned, I got a tattoo of a cross on my back. Every day during my most recent deployment, I prayed Psalm 91 with some of my men; we'd suffered no casualties. I believed in one life, one God, one Heaven. I only had one chance to do things right.

"We aren't soul mates. We were both very young. It's clear now we have nothing in common and very different beliefs."

Robyn's beautiful lips curled. "Maybe you are meant to learn something from each other. We don't always fall in love with someone who is like ourselves. It would be too easy. I'm from a very different background than Xavi. But he completes me, and I've experienced such amazing growth with him. Twenty years together, and we've raised three beautiful children."

I was pleased that their marriage seemed to be the real deal. I had hoped that I wouldn't be paired with a cheating Hollywood housewife who would look at me as if I were a piece of meat.

"You two are fortunate. I hope to find that someday—once I get out of the Marines. But it won't be with Selena."

Robyn put her hand on my knee, but not in a creepy, seductive way. More motherly. "Bret, you can't choose your path. You should just be open to your surroundings." She stood up, walked to the stereo, and turned off the music. Selena and Xavier stopped dancing. Xavier looked as if he might fall to the ground.

"Please, Bret and Selena. Would you both care to join us for lunch?"

Selena gave Xavier an encouraging hug. "Sure. I'm starving."

Robyn led everyone to the redwood deck and then went inside the French doors to bring out lunch. I was also impressed that I hadn't noticed any maids or cooks in the home.

Robyn brought out a pitcher of iced tea, a plate of sandwiches, and a bowl of pasta salad. Everything looked delicious, though I noticed that there was no meat to be found.

I piled my plate. "Thank you, Robyn. You didn't need to do this."

"It's my pleasure. The sandwiches are hummus, avocado, sprouts, and tomatoes, and the pasta is organic, gluten-free, and vegan. Enjoy."

The food tasted great and was surprisingly filling.

We ate quickly and engaged in meaningless conversation about the show. Robyn went to get dessert, and Xavier followed her into the house.

Selena and I stared out into the three-tier rose garden.

"Sorry about earlier. I didn't mean to upset you," I offered.

"It's fine. You made a good point. It's a hard lifestyle for others to accept. I understand. It would be so much easier to be involved with my partner."

"What happened with you and Dima? The truth, please."

Selena pushed the last piece of pasta around on her plate. "What do you want to know?"

The burning question in my head for years couldn't be held back any longer. "Why did you leave me, Sel?"

She looked up at me, her bottom lip trembling. "It's complicated."

The pain was surprisingly as sharp as it had been when I'd received her Dear John letter. "Can't even tell me?"

"Not now, not here." Selena turned to me and placed her hand on my thigh. A warmth shot through my body. She had a tear in her eye, and she didn't even bother to wipe it away.

"Are you going to get back with Dima?"

"I don't think so. I want children. I know Dima wouldn't make a great father. He gets frustrated with kids. You remember how he was with us. Always yelling at us when we made mistakes. Kicking our feet 'til they bled. No patience."

"Dima's abusive. Always has been."

"Not always."

Damn, she didn't even see it. I couldn't handle her defending him. My resentment toward her melted into an emerging protective streak that had never gone away. "You deserve better."

She took a deep breath. "I just don't know what I want anymore. My life is so different since when we were together. I'm different. I was so ugly back then. I hated myself so much. I still do."

My heart broke for her. How did she ever believe that?

"Sel, you were beautiful back then. Perfect. It's this world that makes you feel ugly. But it's fake, not real. I know you, babe. The real you."

She quivered. "You always made me feel beautiful. Thank you for that. And you are right about this world. But I need this title, Bret. I could get kicked off the show tomorrow. My mom sacrificed so much for my dancing lessons. All those competitions and costumes weren't cheap. If I win Blackpool, I'll be able to judge."

A few more tears stained her face. I wasn't sure what to do, but my instinct to comfort her took over. I pulled her toward my chest and just held her.

A rush of feelings came back. I wanted to kiss her but held back.

Was it just nostalgia? Something more? Why did she get to me? It wasn't just looks. She was truly the most beautiful woman in the world. But I knew the girl underneath the extensions, the makeup, the fillers. The only thing I didn't know was if I'd ever truly stopped loving her.

SELENA

After Bret held me the other night, I had hoped that he would ask me out.

But he hadn't.

I wouldn't have been able to see him anyway—I had plans.

Dima was coming to visit.

I took an Uber to the San Francisco airport to meet Dima. He would be judging at the competition, so he didn't come just to see me. I was halfway to the terminal to greet Dima before I realized that I needed to use the bathroom. Darn. I looked at my watch. I was late again. Busting left, I cut around a corner and made a beeline to the restrooms. I ducked into the ladies' room, freshened up, then dashed back out again, making a left in front of the men's room—running smack into two guys making out.

"Oh! Sorry, guys," I mumbled and looked down at my feet, shielding my face from embarrassment. "I totally wasn't looking."

"No worries," I heard. His buddy cracked up, and they ran into the men's room, covering their faces.

No worries?

I know that voice!

I whipped my head back for a look—and saw Eric and some man plowing through the restroom door. Not that I'd needed to see him; I knew Eric's voice when I heard it. Eric, as in *Nicole's husband.*

Good God! The couple with the only perfect ballroom marriage.

He must've been in town for the competition. Where was Nicole? I practically stumbled to the baggage claim, thinking of what I'd just seen.

Eric kissing a *guy?* Nicole would totally freak out if she knew. Or...maybe she *did* know. Oh, God, that was not possible, was it? They were Cinderella and Prince Charming. They were champions *and* had a family.

I needed a drink. I scanned the baggage claim for Dima. No sign of him. Good, I had to process what had just happened.

But this just further strengthened my belief that there were no healthy relationships in the ballroom world.

And I had pushed the desire to be loved away for so long. But I yearned for it now.

The only men I'd ever been with in my entire life were Dima and Bret. Even though Dima and I weren't involved, Dima seemed to think that we would end up together. And though I didn't have any romantic feelings toward him anymore, I felt bound to him. We had joint ownership in dance studios, a clothing line, even endorsement opportunities for fitness products.

Once, it had been all I'd ever dreamed of—ballroom dance, love everlasting, the whole pretty package until Dima dumped me. But now I knew in my soul that it was an unrealistic fantasy that I wanted no part in.

I needed to let Dima know that I was closing the door forever on us.

"Selenichka." Dima greeted me with a kiss on the cheek and a dozen red roses.

Roses? Of course, he brought me roses. He could sense that I was over his manipulation of me and was trying to woo me back. I wouldn't let him.

Dima was definitely trying to woo me. He was dressed in his finest Armani suit. But I would not fall for his charms.

I thanked him for the flowers. "Do you know if Eric and Nicole are going to be at the competition?

"Only Eric. He was on plane together with me and his student. He's judging. Nicole is home in Los Angeles, with the baby. Why you ask?"

"No reason. I just thought I saw him."

We made our way to the curb. A limo Dima had hired whisked us away from the airport.

He tried to put his arm around me, but I pulled away. Dima was unfazed. "Selenichka, this is going to be great weekend."

He had made reservations at my favorite restaurant my favorite vegan restaurant. I ate my weight in hummus, and not once during dinner did Dima make a comment about sticking to my diet. We even drank a rich bottle of Pahlmeyer merlot.

After dinner, we strolled around Fisherman's Wharf. We were recognized by some fans and happily signed a few autographs. But on this night, I wanted Dima all to myself.

We needed to have a talk. The talk.

We made our way to Ghirardelli and ordered huge mugs of hot chocolate and sat inside a booth.

As the warm cocoa coated my throat, I grimaced. Though my chemistry with Dima on the floor was electric, our true feelings toward each other were more familiar than sexy. But I wanted passion, true love.

And more importantly, I could never forgive Dima for the way our relationship started.

I took a deep breath. It was now or never.

But before I could speak, Dima did.

"Selenichka, I've been thinking. I should get back together with you, and we get married."

I almost choked on my hot chocolate. "Married? Are you crazy? We've been broken up for three years, and you want to get married?"

Marriage to Dima was the exact opposite of what I wanted.

"I do. I think it would be good for our result. The judges like to see the couples who marry win."

Well, at least his proposal made sense. I knew he didn't actually want a real marriage. But for a result and control, marriage seemed like a great idea.

To him.

Anger seethed inside me. "For our result? It would help, I know, but that's not a reason to get married. I mean, we're not even dating right now. Does everyone in this business only live their lives to get results? Today, when I saw Eric, he was kissing another man. What does that mean, Dima? Is he gay? Are he and Nicole only married for their result?"

Dima threw up his hands. "Why do I care who it is that Eric kisses? It is none of my business if he is a gay. He is the champion. I don't see how their marriage is important to us."

I knew Dima wouldn't understand my point. "It's not about them. It's about us."

Dima's eyes narrowed. "What are you talking about? I just needed a break from you, but we will end up together, Selenichka. We placed third in Blackpool last year. And Fabio and Gia will retire this year. This is not the time to lose focus. This is our time."

"Forget it." I looked down at my feet.

Dima stirred his cocoa. He lowered his voice. "I love you."

My lips quivered.

I tried another approach. I got up from the table and snuggled next to Dima. "Dimka, I'll always love you. You have been everything to me since I was a little girl. But I want to have kids. And I'm twenty-eight years old. I can't wait forever. I will regret it for the rest of my life if I don't have a family."

Dima clutched my hand. "Maybe after we win Blackpool, we can discuss it."

I didn't want to discuss it. I wanted to end it.

A waiter walked by with a tray full of plates. One of the men at the next table erupted in loud laughter, clapping his neighbor on the shoulder. This wasn't the place to do this. But it *was* the time.

"I'm sorry, but I have to give this back to you." I slipped off my diamond ring. The day he had proposed at the Palace of Fine Arts had been one of the best nights of my life. Back then, I'd still believed in the ballroom fantasy and thought that Dima and I could have it all—success, a family, true love. I was younger then, and we had plenty of time to start a family. But I ached every time I saw a father playing with his kid. No amount of success would be worth the pain of not having a family. And I didn't want to have a family with him.

He grasped the ring. "What does this mean, Selena? You are bound to me. We have contracts, competitions, products, videos, studios. You can't *leave* me. I will wait for you to get ahold of yourself, and we can talk."

"Dimka, we've been broken up for three years. You've been with women during that time. I never went on more than a few dates with anyone." I felt strong. I'd been having doubts for a while and finally had no hesitation about my path. "You'll always be in my life. We can still dance together and work on our projects. I'm grateful for everything you've done for me over the years. But I need to find myself. I don't want to have any regrets."

He pointed his finger at me. "This is about Bret. Have you slept together with him, Selena? Tell to me!"

"How could you ask me that? You and I aren't even dating, and I never cheated on you. *Ever*. I never questioned you about all the rumors with your celebrities. And, not that it is any of your business, but nothing has happened between him and me. This is about *us*. I want a family. I want children. I don't want to marry you."

"Fine. It is over. You won't make the fool out of me." He got up and stormed out of Ghirardelli.

I prayed that no one had taken a picture that would end up in the tabloids.

I could've taken an Uber back to my hotel across the bridge, but I didn't want to be alone. Before I could reconsider, I dialed Bret's number.

"Hey," Bret answered, sounding groggy.

"Bret, I'm stuck in the city. Can you come get me?"

He didn't pause. "Of course. Where are you?"

Selena curled up on the sofa in the houseboat. I had offered to take her back to the hotel, but she asked to hang out with me. Her eyes seemed so sad that I'd relented and invited her in. She hadn't said much on the ride over the Golden Gate Bridge, but I had a suspicion that her state of mind had something to do with Dima. I knew he was in town for the competition.

"I'm sorry, Bret. I shouldn't have called you. I just didn't want to be alone. Thanks for picking me up."

I sat on my father's leather recliner. She was vulnerable, and I wanted to make sure I didn't take advantage of that. "Don't worry about it. I'm always here for you."

She started petting Banjo, who rolled over to get his belly rubbed. "I told Dima that it was over between us personally. Forever. He didn't take it well."

The hair on my arms stood up. Her relationship status shouldn't matter to me. If I let her get too close, she would break my heart again. "I'm sure it was just a fight. Next year, you guys will be back together, planning a wedding. Televised worldwide." I watched her face, expecting her to look confused and lost. But she looked determined, the way she looked before she was about to win a competition.

"No, Bret. Never. We've been broken up for years. And even when we were together, there were rumors about other women. I didn't believe them, but I was never sure. And also . . ." Her face contorted.

"Also what?"

"Never mind."

She was keeping something from me. My best guess was about how she had cheated on me with Dima when I was in boot camp. I was glad she didn't finish— I didn't want to hear about it.

She exhaled and finally continued. "But none of that matters. Dima's a great dancer, but I'm not in love with him. For some reason, I always thought Dima and I would end up back together. Not because we were soul mates or anything. Just because our lives are so intertwined. And I never thought anyone else would want me. I still feel like that ugly, chubby teen who was teased. But you helped me realize that I deserve more than that. I guess what I'm saying is . . . I want you, Bret. Please give me another chance."

Her heart-shaped face glowed in the reflection of the moonlight on the water. My heart beat strongly.

Even after all these years, was it possible that I still loved her?

Selena sometimes had her head in the clouds, but her bright outlook on life softened me. And she was never ugly or chubby to me. She was always perfect. Breathtakingly beautiful. It wasn't just that I was attracted to her; I believed that she was the only one who'd ever really understood me. She was the one who had comforted me when my parents announced they were getting a divorce and when I had been taunted in school for dancing. In boot camp, picturing my future life with Selena had motivated me through the hard times.

But I couldn't, wouldn't risk getting hurt.

"It's late, and you're upset. I'll always be here for you, Selena. As a friend."

She came closer to me. "I don't want to be your friend."

The truth was that my words were empty—I didn't want to be her friend either. The thought of another man, of that motherfucker Dima touching her, made my skin crawl.

"Tell you what, let's crash and talk tomorrow."

She nodded her head. I gave her my bed and slept on the sofa. I didn't want to take advantage of her when she was so emotional.

Over the past ten years, I convinced myself that I had hated dancing, that I hated Selena. But I had allowed my rejection and hurt to cloud my memories.

Dancing with Selena again, experiencing that passion between us, shocked me.

I didn't know if it was because we were in Marin or I had been away from the Marines, but I felt different.

I didn't have a clue what was going to happen with Selena, but I was open to the possibilities.

Xavier bounced across the floor, hitting every beat. He seemed to dance so much better when he danced to his own music. "Work it, Xavi!" I yelled.

Xavier finished his routine and collapsed on the sofa. He was such a wonderful man—sexy, creative, great husband and father. I glanced across the ballroom and watched as Bret and Robyn practiced their samba.

When they finished, Robyn fanned herself. "That's enough. I need some inspiration. Bret, could you and Selena demonstrate how it's done?"

"Of course." I shimmied over to Bret. We hadn't danced together since his audition. But during the past week, I could feel Bret opening up to me. Nothing major, but he seemed to be less judgmental. I even got him to go to a yoga class.

He hadn't kissed me yet, but I could feel the heat of his stare on me.

But I still hadn't told him the truth about what happened between Dima and me when Bret was at boot camp.

I needed to get it off my chest, but I knew Bret would freak. He would probably murder Dima.

I pushed Dima out of my head. I needed to focus on the gorgeous man in front of me.

Electricity pulsed through my body. Touching Bret on the floor, connecting through dance without the awkwardness we shared during his audition, excited me.

I giggled. By looking at him today, no one would ever suspect he could dance at all. His muscular, broad frame hid the smoothness and flexibility of his body. It was like watching an action star do the ballet.

He whispered into my ear, "Why are you laughing, babe?"

"Because you are just so sexy. You don't look like a dancer. At all."

"That's a good thing. No matter what, I'm not waxing my chest. I should've put that in my contract."

"I won't let them." The makeup artists most certainly would try to convince Bret to wax his chest. Sure, all the male dancers' pecs were shiny and bare. What was so wrong with chest hair? Was I the only woman that was turned on by Bret's manly chest? I highly doubted it.

Robyn turned on one of Xavier's hits, a samba. I gyrated my hips, and Bret grabbed me from behind. Gripping my wrist, he spun me into rolls, and our bodies rotated around the floor.

After all these years, Bret was as sharp as ever.

For a second, I allowed myself to indulge in the fantasy of us competing together. Would he ever consider it if we started dating again? Just to make me happy? We could stage a huge comeback. We wouldn't win Blackpool anytime soon, but we could probably win Nationals in a few years. Well, if Dima didn't get a new partner and compete against us.

And even if Dima did, if Bret and I were in love, we could beat Dima. Dima would never love anyone but himself.

The music cut off. Robyn clapped. "You two are brilliant! You should compete."

I was glad that I wasn't the only one thinking we looked great together.

"No way, Robyn. I'm just doing one season, and when it's over, I'm not going to set foot on a dance floor. Except maybe at my wedding someday." He winked at me.

A flatter filled my belly. Was he teasing me? I prayed that he was starting to have feelings for me again.

Robyn's lips curled. "Wedding? Am I missing something? Are you two a hot item?"

I gave Bret a flirty glance. "I wish, but he has friend zoned me. But I do think Bret should consider competing again."

Bret's relaxed face tensed up. "No thanks, Sel. Would be kind of hard, after training my men twelve hours a day. And after this leave, I'm sure we'll deploy again soon. No time for dancing."

My shoulders dropped. But I knew it was a long shot. A girl could dream. For now, I would focus on how I felt when he held me. Would he ever kiss me again?

"Well you two are incredible. Wait here." Robyn ran to the bar and poured champagne in four flutes. She brought them over and handed everyone a glass.

"Okay, here we go," Robyn said. "To our success and journey into the world of reality television. May we be guided by our ancestors. As one of my spiritual teachers once told me, 'When you do what you fear most, then you can do anything.'"

A breathtaking view of the Golden Gate, Bay, and Richmond bridges wowed me as we toasted.

I glanced at Bret and was thrilled that he wasn't even making a face to Robyn's New Age toast.

I raised my glass higher. "I'll drink to that."

"Cheers."

Before I could sip my champagne, Bret pulled me toward him. His mouth covered mine, and when our tongues touched, the taste of him made my body throb. Was this really happening? Ten years later, I was kissing my first love. The girl inside me squealed, the woman inside me hungered for me.

"Yeah!" Xavier exclaimed.

Robyn put her hands in a prayer position and nodded.

I looked up at Bret. "What was that for?"

"I waited ten years to kiss you again, Sel. I didn't want to wait any longer."

We kissed again as the fog crept higher on the world's most beautiful bridges.

Kissing Selena was even better than I imagined and remembered. I couldn't wait to get her alone.

I proposed a weekend getaway to the wine country. And Selena readily accepted.

After checking in and dropping Banjo in the hotel room, we pulled up to Mustards Grill in Napa. My father had often taken me here when I was a boy. It was my favorite restaurant—just good, hearty, all-American food without a hint of pretension.

The drive over had been pleasant. Selena now placed her hand on my leg while I drove, but we still hadn't had the difficult conversation. We had a deep history.

But could we have a future? We were so different. For now, I was enjoying being close to her.

"Bret, I love this place. So rustic. What are you having?"

"The calamari and the hangar steak. And a beer. You?"

Selena perused the menu. "A burger sounds good. I'll have the mushroom and spinach burger."

I laughed. "You realize that's not actually a burger, right? It's made out of vegetables."

"Oh, I know. I just haven't eaten meat in, like, five years."

I sighed. A vision of future dinners made with tofu and tempeh flashed before me. I loved to barbeque chicken, ribs, hot dogs, and burgers with my buddies. But I could be convinced to throw some zucchini on the grill to make her happy.

A waitress stopped by the table and took our orders. She raised an eyebrow when she saw Selena, but if she recognized her, she didn't let on.

We made plans for the weekend. I wanted to take a long bike ride the next morning. Selena wanted to book a couple's massage in the afternoon, which I agreed to as long as I had a female masseuse. I didn't want some dude rubbing his hands all over me.

The waitress delivered the calamari and Selena's salad, with dressing on the side.

I pierced a crunchy calamari ring with my fork and watched as Selena dipped her fork first into the dressing and then scooped up a piece of lettuce.

"What are you doing?"

"Oh, it's a diet trick Vika taught me. Instead of pouring the dressing on your salad, you just dip your fork before every bite."

I shook my head. "You realize how weird you are, right? You weigh barely a buck, and you don't have an ounce of fat on your body. How is a little dressing going to hurt you?"

Selena dipped her fork again. "It's not that simple. Everything shows in the costumes. I just want to be careful. And I ate a bit too much last night with Dima. I was nervous."

"Well, I think you're too skinny. Live a little. Pour that dressing all over your salad."

She looked up at me and smiled. She picked up the little dressing dish and saturated her salad with blue cheese. Her fork scooped up the now soppy greens, and she stuffed them in her mouth. "You're right, it tastes so much better this way."

I laughed.

Selena's eyes scanned the room. Her voice lowered, "Bret, I have to tell you one more thing. About why I broke up with you."

I exhaled. Though I had asked about this the other day, I had come to realize that we were both so young that it didn't matter. I didn't want her to tell me something that would anger me and make me doubt her now. "It's the past, Selena. I know we were really young. Let's just try to move on."

Selena bit her lip. "But I just really need to tell you what happened."

The waitress delivered their meals.

"We were too young. I get it."

Selena's shoulders dropped. "No. You don't. Please. Just listen."

"Sel, it won't change a thing. I know I asked you about it the other day, but I've since decided that it doesn't matter. I'm not going to lie and downplay how much you hurt me, but I just really don't want to discuss it."

"Okay. But we do need to talk about it one day."

"Fine." One day when I was more certain about our relationship, we would have this talk. But I wanted to have a great day, and night, with Selena. Dredging up the past would put me in a bad mood.

We enjoyed the rest of our dinner, and Selena even indulged with me in a hazelnut truffle tart.

After lunch, we went to the couple's massage. I was more relaxed than I had been in years.

And now, I was alone with Selena.

I was a grown man now, not a teen, and definitely not a virgin. But being alone with Sel, after all these years, caused me to feel vulnerable.

My eyes traced her body. I pulled her to me. Her mouth was moist and hot, her lips sweet and soft. She kissed my neck and ran her fingers through my hair. The scent of coconut drove me wild. How could she still smell the same after all these years?

"Bret, you don't know how many times I've dreamt of this moment."

I lifted her up, and she wrapped her legs around me. I carried her to the bed. Her tan skin glistened in the light as I unbuttoned her shirt. A beautiful black lace bra covered her small breasts. I was so glad she had never succumbed to Hollywood pressure and ruined her body with implants.

Selena took off my shirt, her hands running over every inch of my chest, and explored my muscles and tattoos. She found a scar on my back from an explosion that had killed another one of my buddies. I had escaped relatively unscathed, except for some lacerations. Selena didn't ask any details, just kissed my skin.

The last time we had made love, I was just a kid, and though I'd loved her more than anything, I hadn't had a clue what I was doing back then.

Not this time.

I took charge. Kissing her face, her neck, her ears. I was in no rush; all I wanted to do was please her. Exploring every inch of her soft stomach, licking her diamond belly ring. My hands cupped her breasts, and I unhooked her bra, flinging it across the room.

It landed perfectly on Banjo's face, and we both let out a laugh.

"Guess we have an audience." I shooed Banjo away.

My attention turned back to Selena; her rosy nipples waited for my lips. I took one into my mouth, and she moaned. She arched her back, and I kissed, suckled, and nibbled on her. Pleasure swept across her face.

"My turn," Selena said, tugging at my pants.

"Not yet," I grinned. I wasn't done with her.

I took off her skirt and pulled down her matching black lace panties. I couldn't wait to taste her. Kissing her thighs, I first teased her with my fingers. She raised her knees. Her warmth excited me, and I took her sweetness into my mouth, savoring every lick. Selena's breaths grew short and rapid. Writhing on the bed, she placed her hand on the back of his head.

"Bret, oh my God. Please—don't stop."

I had no intention of stopping. Her groans and whimpers were the sexiest sounds. Her hips gyrated, and she climaxed.

After a moment of rest, Selena pushed me to my back and straddled me. "That was amazing," she purred.

She kissed my chest, fondling my shoulders and rubbing her breasts on my stomach. Undoing my belt, she took off my pants and boxers. I relaxed on the bed, and Selena hummed while she teased me with her mouth. She wrapped her lips around me, and I wanted to explode, but I held back. Her sweet mouth was so warm.

After what seemed like an eternity, she released me and curled up by my side.

"Do you have a condom?"

"I thought you wanted kids?" I joked.

Selena laughed. "I do, just not tonight."

"I was kidding." I reached over to my nightstand and grabbed one from my wallet. Selena took it from my hand, ripped it open, and rolled it on me.

I flipped her over onto her back. I paused to take in the beauty of Selena, completely naked, lying beneath me.

Every time I saw her in a magazine or on TV, I had imagined seeing her nude again, for my eyes only.

I kissed her neck and slowly entered her, savoring the moment.

Selena gasped. Her heat clenched around me. She felt so tight, so perfect, so meant for me and me alone.

She grabbed my ass and pulled me toward her until I was so deep that our bodies melted together. I took her harder and faster as she screamed my name over and over.

She wrapped her legs tightly around me, still breathless, and I twisted her around so she could have more control. Selena climbed on top of me, pushing me back on the bed. I propped myself up with a pillow to enjoy the view. Relishing the sight of her riding me, I held her hips, rocking her.

"You're so beautiful, Sel."

I sucked on her nipples, and we came together in perfect sync.

After she pulled away, I held her in my arms. "Selena," I gazed into her eyes, mascara smeared all over her face, "don't leave me again."

She placed her finger over my lips. "I won't."

I closed my eyes for a brief second, never wanting this moment to end.

I awoke the next morning, happier than I'd been in years. Sleeping next to Bret all night, wrapped in his strong arms, I wished we could stay in the bay area forever and never have to return to Hollyweird.

I slipped out of Bret's embrace and peeked at him; he slept peacefully. Last night had been better than even my wildest fantasies. Bret was so strong, so generous, so emotional, so masculine. But one night didn't quell my hunger for him—I now wanted him more than ever, every day for the rest of my life.

Ugh, but it was too soon to even think about that. My only goal was to get through this season.

Rolling out of bed, I snuck past Banjo and threw on my clothes.

But a cloud loomed over my happiness as my anxiety took hold.

Poor Bret had no idea what was in store for him once the tabloids found out that we were now together. Even if I told the truth, I feared the magazines would twist the story into some salacious love triangle, and Bret would be hated as the "other man." There was no way Bret would tolerate being on the cover of every magazine, his honorable reputation tarnished. He'd leave me for sure.

And I hadn't been totally honest with him when we broke up many years ago. I had been withholding a secret from him—a secret that would destroy him.

I had to figure out how to handle this, and fast before I lost Bret forever.

I retrieved my phone from my purse; it blinked with seven missed calls and five texts.

All from Dima.

I stepped onto the patio and called him back.

I whispered so I wouldn't wake Bret. "Hi, Dima."

"Selenichka, where are you? I've been calling to you." His voice was very agitated.

What was I going to tell him? "Uhm, I—"

His voice sounded louder. "Are you there, Selena? I called your room last night, and you were not there."

"It doesn't matter where I am Dima."

"I love you, Selenichka. I know that I said it once to you that I did not want the kids. Please, for you, I will have the children."

"That's sweet, Dima. But we just aren't right for each other."

Dima's voice turned from concerned to irritated. "Are you with Bret? Are you back together with him?"

I didn't want to lie to Dima. And I knew Bret hated lying also. Bret would think if I didn't tell Dima about us, that I was being shady. But if I told Dima the truth, I knew the story would hit the tabloids before the weekend was over.

No. I need to tell the truth.

"Yes, I am." A sinking feeling gripped my chest. What was going to happen now?

A sharp noise came over the phone. Dima must've slammed his fist into something. "Fine, Selena. If this is how you want it. Don't ever think you can come back to me. I *made* you, and this is how you repay to me?"

"Back to you? What are you talking about? We're only partners, Dima, remember. And I'm *still* your partner. We can still dance together."

Dima let out a cocky laugh. "Selenichka, *Zaika*. You are confused if you think I would still dance together with you. I can get any partner in the world. You want this to be over? You think you are too good for me? You knew I would always come back to you. We both needed just a break. Now you don't want me? Okay. It is over. Dancing, too."

My chest constricted. "Over? Are you insane? Blackpool is coming up?"

"We will dance in Blackpool, and then I will find a new partner to dance together with. I will start looking now. Goodbye." The dial tone beeped in her ear.

It was over. Ten years of sacrifice and, in just an instant, my dance career had imploded.

He would find another partner in a minute, and I could never get a partner like Dima again. I was a fantastic dancer and very confident about my abilities. But in ballroom, there were a hundred girls for every guy. And very few guys were the caliber of dancer that Dima was. All of the professional men in the Blackpool Latin final already had partners. If any of them did become available, they would pick a younger girl, not start over with a twenty-eight-year-old woman.

The tears started falling down my face. My career was over.

Bret emerged from the bedroom and walked onto the balcony. "Hey babe, what's wrong?" He put his arms around my waist.

"Just hold me."

Bret hugged me. "You can tell me anything."

I looked into his big blue eyes. When we were kids, we were each other's best friends. We'd known each other's every secret until the end. I longed for that closeness again but was afraid to let him in.

"Uhm, that was Dima. He thought we would get back together romantically, like we've done before. I told him it was over that I was with you. He said that our partnership was over. We are done after Blackpool."

Bret released me and looked away. "What did you expect, Sel? Dima's probably the best male dancer in the world. Once you shut that door for good, of course, he'd bounce. You may have thought you were broken up, but it was always on his terms. As long as you would jump back into his arms whenever he decided the time was right. You know how he works. He's always been involved with his partners. When Carrie cheated on him, that's when he went after *you*. Carrie still wanted to dance with him."

I knew all too well. Carrie had an affair with Giorgio, a gorgeous Italian dancer. When Dima found out, he dumped her even though she begged him to still compete with her.

Even worse, I knew exactly what Dima had done to get me to leave Bret. Luckily, Bret still didn't know the depth of Dima's manipulation.

Yet. I had to tell him.

My lip quivered. It still hadn't crossed my mind that he was going to end our partnership. "I know. But if we win Blackpool in two months, we would have the dance world at our feet. Why would he want to start over?"

"Dancing is his life. Why *wouldn't* he want to start over? If you guys had stuck together, at some point, you would've quit competitive dancing—either because of your age or to start a family. He can dance with a girl in her early twenties and compete for the next ten years. He can win Blackpool in a few months with you, and he'll win Blackpool again with someone else."

Wow, Bret understood Dima better than I did. Maybe it was just because he was a guy.

Bret stared at me. "You aren't regretting leaving him, are you? I don't want you to resent me. This was your choice."

I placed my hand on Bret's face. "No, Bret. I don't. I want this to work with you. I just need to find my way again. All I've ever done is dance and compete."

"Well, I promise I'll do everything to make you happy. Hopefully, you will win Blackpool. At least you can go out on a high note."

As I looked out into the lavender gardens, my mind raced. But Bret helped me relax. He massaged my shoulders and told me what a beautiful dancer I was. How he would support me finding a new partner.

And I knew it would be okay.

Bret scooped me up and started kissing me. He carried me to bed, and we made love.

~

An hour later, Bret hit the shower. I texted Jenny.

Selena: Call me

Bret emerged from the bathroom dressed. He wrapped his arms around me, and the smell of cedar made me giddy.

Bret gazed into my eyes. "I can't tell you how many times I thought of you while I was deployed. You were always on my mind. Of course, it didn't help me that you were on the cover of every magazine."

Over the years, I had received fan mail from many men in the military. I was gracious and would send them an autographed picture and a note back. But I always wondered if any of them served with Bret, and somehow, we'd be able to connect again. "Well, I hoped you would see my pictures from time to time and think of me. I did a few USO shows and always scanned the audience for your face. And when I dressed up in that Marine Corps pinup costume, I was thinking of you. Did you see it?"

A lustful smile broke across Bret's face. "Yeah, I saw it. Every one of my men had it plastered on their rack."

It had never occurred to me how hard it must've been for Bret to see me dressed like that. He'd always been so protective of me. I changed the subject. "What do you want to do today?"

"Let's go on a hike."

"Sounds fun. Can you go get some coffee while I get ready?"

"Sure. I'll go to the one down the street. Banjo needs a walk anyway." He kissed me, leashed up Banjo, and left the room.

I figured the cafe would be packed with the weekend breakfast crowd, so I'd have time to take a relaxing bath. And unlike when I was shooting, I was on a small getaway. No need to rush.

I took a wine bottle and a glass, went into the bath-room and drew myself a bubble bath. Just as I was about to jump in, the phone rang.

"Pardon me, bubbles," I said giddily, "I'm being summoned." Having a day off was rough—normally, I'd already be by Dima's side, teaching students for the competition.

I grabbed my phone on the third ring. "*Hola?*"

"Hey, Sel."

I jerked the phone away from my ear. Jenny talked loud even on the phone. "Hey girl. I'm so glad you called. You won't *believe* what happened. Dima wanted to get back together and get married. But I told him it was over forever. And now he won't dance with me. We are done after Blackpool."

"Shut up! You did not."

"Yes, I did. I should've done this years ago. He's been hooking up with every celebrity partner on the show for the past few years. How could he expect me to wait around?" I leaned into the bathroom to see if my bubbles were going down. Nope. The queen's bath was still royal.

"Are you serious?" Jenny's voice changed from her girlfriend-friendly into her professional nagging tone. "What about the studios? Your endorsements? Selena —are you thinking at all?"

"Yes, I'm thinking." I stopped ogling the bubbles.

"I can't believe this! Are you sure this has nothing to do with Bret? Don't lie to me, Selena."

"Well, maybe." I poured myself a glass of Chardonnay. "Fine—we did hook up last night."

"Hooked up? Selena! Did you sleep with him?"

I nearly dropped the Chardonnay bottle. "Yes. It was amazing! He's incredible."

"Oh my God—I need details! What are you going to do now?

"I don't know. You can't tell a soul until I figure this out. No one can know. I don't want the tabloids to find out and ruin Bret's life." But I knew that it didn't matter. Dima would tell the world.

There was a big sigh on the other end of the phone. I tightened my towel and looked longingly at my bath.

"Are you going to tell Bret what happened with Dima when he was in boot camp?"

It was my turn to sigh. "Yes, of course, I am. I tried, but he didn't want to talk about it."

There was no talking Jenny down a tree once she'd climbed it high enough. "Fine, Selena. But you need to tell him soon if you want this to work out."

"I know. I'll figure it out."

Jenny was the only person I had told about what happened when Bret left for the Marines. I was engaged and madly in love with him. Dima had just broken up with Carrie. He was pressuring me to leave Bret, but I refused.

Until one night.

"Selena, are you still there? You realize your competitive career is over, don't you?"

She was right. "Of course, I do." But I didn't want to deal with it. I considered dropping the phone in the bath and pretending I got disconnected.

Luckily, Jen's tone changed. "I'm still happy for you, Sel. But you better make sure there are no paps around, or it will be all over *TMZ*."

My bubbles were popping in the tub. Enough waiting. I took the phone to the bathroom and slipped into the foamy heaven. *Ah, bebita.* This was the life. "Don't worry," I said, settling in, "we'll make sure to keep a low profile."

"Sounds good. I'll let you know if Dima starts running his mouth. You need to get Dima to agree to release a statement. And you need to tell Bret as soon as possible."

"Okay, okay." I lifted a pile of bubbles on my palm. "I'll catch you later. Love ya, kisses."

"Yeah, love you, bye."

I turned on the tap to let in more hot water then sank lower into the glorious warmth.

I blew the bubbles off my palm and watched the glistening cloud float to the water. Maybe after Blackpool, I could take a few months off and enjoy life. I would practically *kill* for a heaping plate of chorizo nachos with mounds of guacamole, sour cream, olives, and cheese, not to mention chicken mole verde and my mom's fresh homemade pumpkin empanadas. My nana made the best empanadas ever. The meal-plan Dima had me on was horrible: egg whites, spinach, tofu, and veggies. That was it. At least the chef I had was great.

"And I *chose* that?" I muttered to my bubbles. "What an idiot." Maybe Bret was right. How about a normal life? What would that be like? Falling in love and not worrying about choosing between him and my career. And starting a family. I would love to spend my days playing with my kids at the park.

Ooh, and drinking Starbucks Venti Caramel Frappuccinos *with* whipped cream, and eating plates and plates of Round Table's King Arthur Supreme Pizza with shrimp and anchovies, and *inhaling* chocolate pecan pie a la mode and Pina Coladas without reporting to barre classes five minutes later. And letting my natural hair color grow out. That would be something. I hated being blonde. I was Latina—it wasn't right. I could also stand not being a tanorexic. And how about saving the lives of the minks who had died for my fake eyelashes. And a vacation, what was that like?

I wanted to find out. I wanted to live my life my way.

I wanted a life off-camera, period.

I scooped up bubbles with both hands and lifted them to my face, staring into a billion sudsy prisms. I loved the glimpse into this world that Bret had. I wanted more.

Hell, I *deserved* more.

The bathroom light twinkled in the suds.

Yeah, I could stand this life.

I closed my eyes, made my wish, and blew hard.

BRET

We arrived back in Los Angeles three days before the first show. There was so much to do—Selena had begun the process of separating her businesses from Dima, as I was preparing for my time in the spotlight.

I pulled the truck in front of Selena's house. I scanned the driveway—no Lamborghini in sight. Dima must've been hiding out somewhere.

"You sure you want to go in by yourself? I can stay with you, just in case Dima comes back."

Selena gave me a warm kiss. "No, babe. It's okay. I doubt Dima will show up. He's probably auditioning his next partner. I'll be fine."

"Okay. But call me if Dima shows up. Or if you need anything. I'll only be two hours away so I can come back if you need me to."

Banjo licked Selena's face, and, for once, she didn't immediately wipe off his slobber. "I'll miss you, too, Banjo. Call me later, Bret."

I headed down the hills. I hadn't been away from Selena for longer than a dog walk since we'd gotten back together. I needed some time to process everything that had happened.

I pulled to the side of the road and made a call.

Ray picked up on the first ring. "Hey, stranger. I thought you went UA. How've you been?"

"Good. You know there's nothing unauthorized about this absence. Though I have considered taking off to Canada—to escape this show, not the Corps. But I'm back in southern California. What are you doing tonight? Can I buy you a beer?"

A baby cried in the background. "Man, Nia went to her sister's house. I'm watching the kids. Tell you what, bring over some beer and pizza, and we'll catch the UFC match."

"Sounds like a plan. I'll be over in about two hours."

It sounded like the perfect night to me: my best friend, my dog, watching guys beat each other up, beer, pizza, and no cameras anywhere.

~

"Uncle Bret!" Ray's three boys were waiting in the driveway when I parked.

"Is this your truck?" Jackson, Ray's twelve-year-old, seemed hypnotized by the headlights.

"No, buddy. It's just on loan. I have to give it back soon."

Jackson's shoulders slumped. "Man, that sucks."

I doled out gifts to the boys. I'd bought them bars of Ghirardelli chocolates and toy cable cars.

Ray appeared at the doorway, holding his baby daughter. "Nice truck. Did congress give us a raise I don't know about? I thought you were giving all the money on the show to Pierce's family? Keep spending like that, and you won't have anything left."

I grabbed the pizzas, beer, and sodas. "Haven't touched the money. Ford gave me this truck for a promotion. I tried to refuse it, but I'm stuck with it. I'll sell it after the show."

A wrinkle crossed Ray's face. "Seriously? They gave you this truck, and you want to return it? Are you nuts? Give it to me. Man, you should get *something* for making a jerk out of yourself. I can't wait to see you on television next week. I know you're gonna get me some free tickets."

"I get two free tickets to every show. You want to come?" I hadn't planned on inviting Ray, mostly out of pure embarrassment.

"Hell yeah! We'll be there. Wouldn't miss it for the world. How about in three weeks—I have duty next week, and that will give us time to find a babysitter."

"Sure. I'll put you on the list."

I led Banjo to the backyard and let him run around. For base housing, this place was pretty nice: four bedrooms, two-and-a-half baths, two-car garage, laundry room, and a small yard. But no matter how hard I tried, I couldn't picture Selena ever living on base with me, in a modest home like this.

The boys each took a slice of pizza and a soda and then went out back to play fetch with Banjo. Ray placed the baby in her swing and settled into the sofa. I took a slice of pizza, sat in a chair, and waited for the UFC match to begin.

Ray eyed me. "So, how's it been?"

I was relieved to have someone to talk to. "Not too bad. Do you know who Robyn Quintana is? She's my partner."

"Are you serious? She's *fine*. Nia will freak. She loves her. Is she cool?" Ray took out his phone and texted his wife.

"Yeah. She's cool. I mean, totally loopy. She believes in past lives and all that stuff. But she's down-to-earth. A good mom. I lucked out."

"We get to meet her when we go to your show?"

"Of course. She's a good dancer. I don't think we'll get eliminated."

Ray paused and checked his phone. "Nia is stoked." Ray took a sip of his beer, his eyes dancing. "So how's your ex? You hit that yet?"

I took a sip of my own beer. "Yup."

"Ahh, I knew it, dawg. I told Nia that you had no self-control. Not that I can blame you—she's slammin'."

I couldn't believe that I had ever thought I'd be able to resist Selena. "You were right. I didn't think it would happen at all, ever. She's a spoiled princess. But we started hanging out together, and she's no longer dancing with Dima. So, yeah, you could say we're back together."

Ray just laughed. "Man, you're crazy. I mean, that's cool and all. I can't blame you. But think with your head. You're still a Devil Dawg. Selena's not cut out for this life—and you know it. What if your next orders are to the east coast? Are you going to do long distance? Give up that Hollywood lifestyle for life on the base? I mean, we have rats in our house. Rats! I called housing, and they said they were going to look into it. She doesn't fit in here. Enjoy the ride, but if it explodes in your face, remember I'll be here for you."

I wasn't even annoyed; I knew Ray was right.

I changed the subject. "So, who's fighting tonight?"

"It's gonna be great. Rogelio Viramontes is taking on Josh Cutler. Rogelio is a former jarhead."

"Awesome." I relaxed and tried to clear my mind of Selena and the show. I didn't need money, a nice truck, a beautiful house. I was happy just hanging out with my best friend, my brother-in-arms, and enjoying life.

I looked over at his baby, and she gave me a goofy grin. I envied Ray's life—kids, a beautiful wife, a stable home life. Did Selena want the same things as I did?

I couldn't let go of the nagging feeling that she would never be satisfied with my life, or with me.

I studied myself in the mirror before I took the stage for the show's season premiere. I frowned and shook my head.

"I hate this outfit, Sel."

Selena laughed.

I was dead-on about this costume. An open, lemon-and-lime-colored silk shirt with orange feathers sprouting out of my arms—I looked like the mutant offspring of a parrot and a bottle of Squirt soda. If I started flapping, I'd probably lift right off the ground.

"Yeah, you do kinda look like you might fly away," Selena admitted as she walked over to the stereo and turned on the music for Robyn and me. "But, no, it's good. Very traditional mambo. The judges will love it."

"At least someone will. I'll never hear the end of this. They'll be calling me Staff Sergeant Peacock." I shrugged. "Well, at least my partner looks beautiful, even if she's also covered in feathers. One more time?" I grabbed Robyn's hand.

We started to dance our routine on the small black practice floor behind the main set. Xavier and Selena ran through some steps for their routine. A couple of random key grips and assistants roamed around.

Robyn was a perfectionist. She was the one always asking for one more practice round—my dream celebrity partner. And she could totally dance.

Robyn's face lit up. She twisted and shook to the music in perfect beat.

We just might win. Then this nightmare show will be worth it.

The music abruptly stopped.

"Hey!" I snapped.

Dima was at the corner of the practice floor, changing the track. "Oh, I'm so sorry, guys. Were you not done?

Here, I'll put it back on for you." He flashed a dirty look at Selena.

I needed to get through my first night without a confrontation.

"No thanks, Dima, we're all done." I extended my hand. "Good luck tonight."

"Okay. See you guys out there." Dima squinted, and then suddenly smiled like he was plotting something. He took the hand of his teen celebrity partner, Laura. "*Ni pukha, ni pera,*" he tossed our way as I ushered Robyn toward the red room.

Robyn cast a confused glance toward Dima. "What was all that 'pookie knee parrot' stuff? What did he say?"

Selena answered. "It's like break a leg in Russian. It actually means 'neither down from a duck, nor feather.'"

"Duck? Who's he callin' a duck?" she cried, straightening her back and adjusting her fluffy yellow costume. "I'll have you know, I'm a bona fide canary."

I laughed. "Oh, see, and here I was thinking parrot."

Xavier turned toward Selena. "So, you speak Russian, too?"

"No. But I understand a lot. You have to in my line of work."

We all headed back to the red room, the official back-stage viewing area. Sparkly gold valances adorned the walls, and an opulent crystal chandelier blinded me as I entered. Jenny sat on one of the brown velvet couches, hugging a red pillow as if it were her teddy bear. Soothing ballroom music streamed in from the overhead speakers.

But the noise wasn't enough to drown out Selena and Dima, who began ripping into each other. Again.

"I told to you that my lawyer will distribute your money," Dima snapped.

"Dima, you put a hold on our business bank account. I can't believe you did that!"

No way would Dima be stupid enough to lose his temper with the cameras on and me standing there. "Selena, we will handle this later."

Selena gave me a "please don't get involved" look. But I couldn't resist.

"Hey." I put my hand on Dima's shoulder. "Why don't you just cut her a check for now and let the lawyers deal with it later. There's no need to be a jerk."

Dima turned his charm on me as a cameraman approached. "Sure, friend. Sounds good."

She just turned around, grabbed a brush from her bag, and started scaling the suede sole on her shoe.

When her soles were brushed out, Selena put her arm around me. "You nervous?"

"No. I just hope none of my Marines are watching this."

"Ha! Don't worry. I think you're safe. They don't know you're on the show yet. I doubt a bunch of Marines are crowded around a television set in Fallujah, watching *Dancing Under the Stars*. Isn't *Monday Night Football* on?"

A director ran through the door. "Okay, everyone, five-minute warning for the opening."

A makeup girl started brushing my face with foundation as I winced.

A costume assistant eyed me suspiciously. "Do you think he's stoned enough?" she asked Kendrick, the costume designer.

"Absolutely not. More stones. *More stones!*" Kendrick pushed Selena off of me and attacked me from behind with a Bedazzler and shot me up with more rhinestones. I didn't know whether to duck or cover.

"Are you nuts, Kendrick?" I asked. "I already have fifteen thousand stones on this outfit."

"Fifteen thousand and *one*, fifteen thousand and *two...*" Kendrick counted as he blinged me up. This guy didn't mess around. Kendrick had already made sure my shirt was cut open because it was more flattering for "someone with my manly chest," after I had won my battle to keep my chest hair. Thoughtful guy, that Kendrick.

As Kendrick bedazzled me, I made sure to breathe.

When he was done, Selena rubbed my back. "Are you ready?"

"Not sure. This is serious. I don't think I can go out there and humiliate myself." My hands shook.

Selena rummaged behind the sofa, found her purse, and handed me a flask.

I took a gulp of whiskey, hoping it would calm me down.

She whispered in my ear, "You'll be fine, babe. You won't humiliate yourself. And before you know it, this season will be over."

I pursed my lips until they turned white. I prayed I wouldn't screw up so I could get enough money for Pierce's family. After all they had been through, even dancing dressed up like a peacock was worth it.

"Live, from Hollywood, it's *Dancing Under the Stars!*" the British voiceover said on the other side of the curtain like the Wizard of Oz. The audience screamed and clapped on cue.

"C'mon, soldier, suck it up," Dima hissed.

"I'm a Marine, asshole."

But Dima was right. This was no time to be coddled. I was a former champion; I could do this.

Dima shoved his partner ahead of me. The annoying theme song started playing, and the pros marched out one by one with our partners. We all arrived on the floor, and the camera panned across our beaming, nervous faces. Selena started bopping along to the music. Vika blew kisses at the audience. Robyn popped on her most beautiful smile. And I stood up straight like I was in formation.

It was showtime.

The host, Matt Brinkman, was in his glory. "This is our best year yet with Olympic medalists, Grammy Award winners, and reality and network television stars! And we also have a new professional dancer. This is your first chance to see our competitors. Now for our first dancer, Emmy-winning television star Robyn Quintana!"

I presented Robyn to the audience to a roar of applause. "Robyn is the star of the long-running daytime soap *Delicious Divas*," Brinkman said. "She's won seven daytime Emmys. Robyn is paired with our newest professional dancer, American War Hero Bret Lord."

American War Hero? Who wrote that? My cheeks flushed.

The overhead monitor cut to a clip of Robyn and me as the rest of the dancers scurried back to the red room to watch our montage and our performance.

"I'm Robyn Quintana, and I'm the star of *Delicious Divas*. I'm also a wife and mother." Her charm bounced off the TV screen. Clips of her television shows graced the screen.

"I'm Bret Lord, and I'm a former amateur United States National Latin Champion. I'm currently a staff sergeant in the United States Marine Corps." I looked at the screen and saw competition footage of Selena and I winning our championship, and then later on the road trip in the truck, talking about Pierce. A short segment played of my Marine unit, with me yelling at my men in formation. I had told my men that the cameramen were just filming a documentary about the Marines.

The audience let out a collective gasp as the reel flashed a picture of Pierce's funeral, his wife and young children walking behind the casket.

A single tear threatened to slip from the corner of my eye, but the cameras were luckily not on me.

There it was—no more hiding. By morning, every member of my unit would know where I had disappeared to over the last month.

Another clip showed the first time I met Robyn in Tiburon.

The voiceover cut in: "Dancing the mambo, Robyn Quintana and her partner, United States Marine Bret Lord."

Now live, I led Robyn to the floor. "Mambo #5" started playing. I twirled her around, and she was on fire. It was a fun routine with a lot of basic actions to please the judges. I moved my hips, and Robyn shimmied around me, swishing the matching citrus-colored fringe of her two-piece dress. She swiveled in front of me, and I shook my chest. Our energy rippled through my body. We crashed our hips together and rolled off each other, never losing eye contact. I spun her into me and dipped her to the ground.

The crowd roared.

My heartbeat raced. I hadn't made a fool out of myself, and I was one step closer to providing for Pierce's family.

"Excellent job. The ballroom is on fire tonight," Matt said. "That's how it's done. And Bret, thank you for your service. Let's see what the judges have to say. Benjamin Brooks?"

The camera panned to Benny, who wore a yellow suit, black silk shirt, and his signature bolo tie. He looked like a bumblebee. Benny rose to fame at a time when ballroom dancing consisted of stringing together a series of cheesy poses while the men paraded around in ruffled white catsuits that were split in a long V shape to ensure that their excessive manes of chest hair showed.

"Robyn, it was a beaut'. You have rhythm, charm, and a bonzer of a body. Well done."

"Karen Brooks Lopez," Matt said, "what did you think of Robyn and Bret's mambo?"

Karen leaned on her ex-husband. "Robyn, you were superb. I'm so impressed with what Bret has taught you."

"Steve Samson, your thoughts?" Matt asked.

Steve Samson was single-handedly responsible for getting ballroom dancing on television. In the nineties, he ran and was the commentator on a successful television show on PBS, *The Turquoise Pendant Ball*. The entire dance industry was grateful to the exposure he had given ballroom dancing. As progressive and flamboyant as he could be, Steve provided a great contrast to Benny's old-school traditional views on ballroom.

"Robyn, what a looker. Your spicy exoticism captivated me."

The audience simultaneously rushed to their feet and clapped wildly.

We rushed backstage and waited for our scores. The judges gave us straight nines! A twenty-seven for our first show.

All of my hard work had paid off. What had only been a dream months ago was finally coming true. I was proud that I had made the sacrifice to go on this show.

A costume assistant came out of nowhere, pulled me behind the red room, and started ripping off my clothes. I had almost forgotten I had to dance a demonstration with Selena. The makeup girl powdered my face despite my protests. She smudged some lipstick on my lips, and before I could blink, she threw me back onstage.

"Now, ladies and gentlemen," Matt said. "We're going to start with a rumba demonstration from Season Twenty-Four winner, Selena Martinez, and our newest professional, Bret Lord."

The band started playing a rumba, "I Just Can't Stop Loving You," by Michael Jackson.

I crept up behind Selena and took her arm. We slid into the rumba, and I pulled her to my chest. My white billowy shirt was only partially unbuttoned. Selena caressed my neck and gave her body over to me. I grasped her waist, and she rolled down my body. It felt like we had never stopped dancing years ago. But it was even better than I had remembered. The tension between us was electric. I craved her. She ran away from me and teased me with fleeting views of her inner thighs. The song started to taper, and I took her into my arms.

When the lights died down, and the stage was completely dark, I gave her a kiss on the lips. I didn't care who saw us.

The lights came back on, and the crowd erupted.

Did I really kiss her? No one saw for sure. And if they had, I didn't care. Selena was in my arms—just like old times.

Xavier and I stood nervously onstage next to Eric and his partner, reality star Aubrey, awaiting our fate. Last night, Bret and Robyn had received an amazing score in the mambo, so they were safe. But someone was about to get the ax.

"And the couple leaving us tonight—Eric and Aubrey," Matt said.

Xavier gave me an excited hug. We would live to dance another week.

After the usual onslaught of interviews, Eric and Aubrey hopped into a limo to take them to the airport. They were booked on the redeye to New York for the losers' round of morning talk shows.

Dima had cut me a check for some expenses. Even so, we hadn't had a real conversation since he'd ended our dance partnership. But he had agreed to a joint statement, which our publicist released last Friday afternoon—after all the tabloids had already gone to press.

"We have been partners on and off the floor for ten years. Unfortunately, we have come to the conclusion it would be in our best personal and professional interests to end our partnership after this year's Blackpool Competition. We will stay close friends and coworkers. There were no third parties responsible for the split, and we ask for your respect and privacy during this difficult time."

Selima was dead. Our agent had tried to convince us to wait until the season was over to announce our split, but I had refused. If Bret wasn't in the picture, I would've agreed to pretend, but I wasn't going to jeopardize my newfound happiness.

That evening, Dima and I had been scheduled to dance a show for our studio. But because we'd broken up, Vika offered to dance in my place. Which meant that tonight, I could spend the entire night with Bret and not have to worry about dealing with Dima.

Backstage, Jenny rushed over with my phone and purse in hand. "I can't believe we made it! One more week. I thought for sure this time I'd be gone. Let's go celebrate. Here."

My phone flashed as Jenny handed it to me.

Bret*:* Meet me at my hotel room in one hour.

Elizabeth came bounding up from behind. She gave Jenny a big hug. "See! I told you everything would be fine. Where do you guys want to go? I want to have a girls' night. Let's go to Nobu. I'm craving abalone."

I stashed my phone in my purse. "You guys go ahead. I'm not in the sushi mood." The reporters started exiting, so we moved to the side of the stage.

"Fine, no sushi. Let's go to The Ivy." Jenny picked up her phone and started dialing. "Not a raw fish in that place."

I winked at Jenny. "Not tonight, Jen. I'm super tired. I have an early drive to San Francisco tomorrow, so I'm gonna just go home so I can get some sleep."

Jenny knowingly nodded, but Elizabeth was so happy-happy-joy-joy she didn't give it a second thought.

"Then it's just Jen and me," Elizabeth chirped. "Sel, you call us later. I need to par-*tay*!"

"Oh, God," Jen muttered as Elizabeth pulled her over to the lingering media. "We've created a monster, Sel," she called over her shoulder.

I shrugged and gave her a thumbs-up, watching them disappear around the corner with the reporters.

Bingo! Exit, stage right!

Jenny was right, though—just last season, Elizabeth had never set foot inside a dance club. Life as a Mormon is wild, isn't it? When we hit the clubs in Cabo, Elizabeth ordered sparkling water. Sometimes, when she really cut loose, she'd add a slice of lime. And no Starbucks? Where was the joy in *that*? Jenny and I had vowed not to corrupt her; I respected Elizabeth's lifestyle and religion. Elizabeth reminded me of myself at eighteen—madly in love with Bret, worshipping Dima, and unaware of a world outside the dance studio. I just hoped that Elizabeth was stronger than I had been back then.

But I wasn't eighteen anymore—I was a grown woman, and I couldn't wait to be alone with Bret.

I ducked out the back of the studio, called my driver, and told him to meet me in forty-five minutes.

I rushed to my trailer across the back lot and shimmied out of my dress before the door had even closed. *Shower!*

Scrubbing the orange tanning cream off myself under the hot water, I marveled for the millionth time that a Latina had to paint her skin like some kind of coloring book. It was the dumbest thing ever—and God, did I hate the smell of the stuff. I nearly grafted my skin trying to loofah it off, but I still had orangey running streaks all over my body. I swore I looked like a stubby giraffe. I slathered on Palmer's Cocoa Butter to mask the smell. Sure, I could afford the expensive creams and all now, but I loved my Palmer's, so it stayed. My mane of hair was all over the place, so I scrunched in some spray gel and stuffed it under a big, floppy hat.

Just as I finished up, my phone vibrated.

Twenty-three new messages? What the heck?

Half of them were from Jenny—in the past twenty minutes. What was her problem? I'd already told her I didn't want to hang out.

> **Jenny:** Sel, check this out
>
> **Selena Martinez Cheater**

Oh no.

I clicked on the link.

> Not So Blind Item
>
> Which *Dancing Under the Stars* hoofer recently dumped her partner for her ex? This *spicy* salsa queen seduced the newest professional dancer on his debut season. Developing…
>
> **3 COMMENTS**:
>
> **DUTS addict:** it's that slut Selena Martinez.
>
> **Reina Rumba:** Can't blame her! Bret's fine.
>
> **Dima's lover:** Dima's better off without her.

How did the gossip sites know *everything*? I'd been back together with Bret for less than two weeks. I hadn't told anyone other than Jenny. Someone must have seen us. Maybe it was that room service guy—he had looked at us funny yesterday morning when he'd delivered our breakfast. Or the waitress at Mustards? What would Bret say?

Or . . . it was Dima.

Yes. It *had* to be. Dima loved the limelight and wouldn't waste a chance to paint himself as the victim.

That bastard.

What if Bret left me because of the gossip? Or my fans believed I cheated on Dima even though we hadn't been dating?

I took a deep breath. I needed to calm my ass down. I knew this was going to happen. I just didn't think I would have to deal with it so soon.

I wonder if… I leaned toward the window in my trailer and peered outside. *They are!*

There were at least thirty paparazzi on the sidewalk outside the lot with video cameras and those long extender things.

Wait, was that one guy pointing the lens at this window?

Flashes went off.

I slammed the curtains shut.

I was trapped.

My driver was due to pick me up now.

Think.

I poked my head out of the door and looked down both sides of the backlot. Coast was clear. Thank god for our security. The *Mission Impossible* theme song played in my head as I slinked through the door. Super quickly, I ran through the maze to the garage. No cameras.

But my celebration was short. When I got to the garage, my driver wasn't in sight.

I texted him again, hoping the voices around the side of the building weren't the paps. But of course, they were. *Driver, where are you?*

The cameras started going off as my limo cruised down the parking ramp. I ran to the car while it was still moving and pounded on the door for the driver to unlock it.

"Girl, you trying to get yourself killed?" he asked.

"That would be one solution." I scrambled into the limo and reached for the Don Julio Blanco bottle. I took a swig of tequila, straight out of the bottle. Who needed the glass? "Sorry about all that. Just take me to the hotel. Fast. And try to lose those guys on our tail."

The tires busted outta there. "Aye, aye, boss!" he squealed, yahooing for good measure.

I left the glass in the rack and continued chugging from the bottle.

Another text appeared.

Mom: Are you back with Bret?

Oh Lord. My mom wanted me to stay with Dima for the financial security and, as she'd once said, "to not be a broke military wife."

I couldn't deal with her right now.

The driver turned onto the street of the hotel. Dammit. There were more paps waiting in the lobby. I almost told my driver to take off again, but I didn't know if I could survive another mile with this Mario Andretti wannabe.

Breathe, Sel. You can do this...

I put on my oversized Chanel sunglasses and opened the limo door before the driver could get there.

Immediately, a *TMZ* reporter shoved a camera in my face. "Selena, are you having an affair with Bret?"

I pushed past him to the steps. A hundred feet more, and I would be safe.

A *Star* writer blocked the entrance. "Selena, Selena, is it true that Dima walked in on you and Bret having sex backstage on the show?"

Are you kidding me?

"What do you have to say for yourself?"

Get a life! That's what I have to say. "I don't know what you're talking about. Bret and I are just friends, and we've known each other for over twenty years. Dima and I haven't been in a romantic relationship for three years. We just ended our dance partnership. There is *no* scandal. Please leave me alone."

I headed into the elevator. The ride up took forever. Fifth floor...sixth floor...seventh floor. *Ding!* I stepped off.

Breathe, baby.

Room 715...717...719... I looked to the next door and spotted Bret, looking sexy as all hell wearing Calvin Klein pajama bottoms and no shirt, wedged in the doorway, waiting for me.

But before I could do or say anything, he seized me, pulling me into the brightly lit room, and started kissing my neck.

"What took you so long?" He clasped my hands in his.

"The paparazzi. They know about us."

"Who cares? Come here." He tossed me down on the bed.

I rolled on top of him. Our bodies were made for each other. He slowly undressed me, taking his time exploring my body. We kissed for what seemed like forever, just like when we were fifteen years old.

"I love you, Selena."

Euphoria pulsed through me. "I love you, too."

"You smell even sweeter than I remember," he whispered.

Another star for Palmer's Cocoa Butter.

I had to be camera-ready in forty-five minutes to film the new fitness video, *Dancing Under the Stars: Cardio Tango.* How incredibly lame was that? What was a Cardio Tango anyway? And with the gossip about me everywhere, I would rather do anything but this.

Bret left the hotel early this morning to take a day off. I couldn't blame him.

I bolted out of bed, tripping on the comforter and landing on my butt.

Good God, almighty! I stood up and looked at myself in the mirror. My hair was all matted together like cotton candy. I couldn't even get a comb through it. I whipped through my patented ten-minute beauty routine—showered, put on deodorant, brushed my teeth, and lathered some conditioner through my hair, then wrapped it in a towel. Thank God they had makeup people on set. I threw on some sweats and grabbed my purse.

I texted my driver to meet me in the service garage then headed for the door, taking one last glance in the mirror. Oh, good Lord—I still had the towel wrapped around my hair. I reached up to take it off but stopped myself; I'd look like a babushka just in case anyone saw me. Perfect disguise. The towel stayed.

Luckily, there were no cameras to be found, and I slid out the back door of my hotel and found my driver.

Six minutes later, he pulled up to the studio. A few cameras lingered outside, but I just shoved past them. It took all my strength to plow through the front door.

The other girls were sitting on the couch in the lobby in matching blue and white dance shorts and halter-tops, like a trashy version of the Dallas Cowboys Cheerleaders. Nicole had her arms draped around Vika, with Jenny sitting close. Strangely, Elizabeth had removed herself from the group and was at the other end of the couch.

Jenny hustled over to me. "How are you? Stupid tabloids." She put her arm around my shoulders and ushered me away from the paps in the window. "Don't worry, Sel, it'll all blow over. I told everyone it's not true." She winked at me. Jenny always had my back.

Time to come clean. I didn't want Jenny to have to lie for me.

Vika walked over to me. "So, it is true? You dumped Dima?"

I stepped from Jenny's side and faced Vika. I could understand why Vika was upset. Though we weren't as close as Jenny and I were, Vika and I had become like family when I was with Dima. She had always assured me that Dima loved me, and we would end up together.

"Vika, I..." I still had my sunglasses on. I couldn't face them yet. "I..." Oh, God, they could all see right through me. I couldn't lie to Vika's face. "I...I'm sorry, but it's true. I'm with Bret."

Vika let out a gasp. "Dima told to me that he wanted to get back together with you, but you dumped him because he didn't want the kids," Vika said, getting up from the couch and walking straight at me.

"That's not true. But Vika...Dima and I have been broken up for years. I didn't want to get back together with him, so he ended the partnership. It really has nothing to do with me dating Bret."

Vika stabbed her finger at the paps through the window. "*I* actually defended you to the sleazy reporters." She straightened up and set her jaw. "You're so stupid, Selena. No one will ever dance together with you again."

Every word was like a rock to my head.

"Do you hear me, you...you...you and that stupid towel on your head!"

My chest tightened. I never wanted this to happen.

Elizabeth tried to sneak out of the lobby, motioning Jenny to escape with her. But Jenny stayed put on the sofa, seemingly hypnotized by the drama. Elizabeth sat back down.

I didn't know what else to say. So I said nothing.

Vika looked up. Her normally blue eyes were now a piercing shade of turquoise. The blinding lights of the cameras were still going off, trying to snap a picture of Vika and me. The ambulance chasers! As if this situation wasn't bad enough...as if I had actually done something wrong! I'd never cheated on Dima. It was the other way around.

Vika and those baby doe eyes—she'd cheat on Benny in a heartbeat if she thought she could find someone else to take care of her.

"Dima gave you his world, and now you have nothing."

I snapped.

"Dima cheated on me for years. And he got me drunk and took advantage of me when I was with Bret. Dima screwed me over!"

She gasped. "Liar! Dima never would do that."

"He did! So what that I'm with Bret? Hell, Vika, you're married to a man old enough to be your grandpa just to get to the top. Don't you see this is different? I love Bret. *I love him.* And I don't care if Dima hates me. He cheated on me. He hurt me. But I love Bret. And Bret loves *me.*"

She smiled grimly. "Well, I hope you are happy. Now you don't even have partner."

"Enough!" Nicole blurted. She shook her head at Vika.

Nicole was always good to me. I hoped that she and Eric at least had some kind of agreement, and she wasn't getting cheated on.

Vika looked at her feet. "I'm sorry, Selena."

"It's fine." I just wanted the drama over.

Nicole's eyes narrowed, then she turned to Vika. "C'mon, luv, let's go clean up. We still have to film this video." She took Vika by the hand and led her out of the lobby. I watched them go.

Elizabeth leaped off the sofa with a crooked smile on her face, like she'd just come to some profound realization. "Don't worry, Selena. Everything will be okay. You did what you had to do. Nothing works out perfectly in the ballroom world." She smiled and pranced out of the room.

Elizabeth was a sweetheart. I hoped that she would never succumb to the jerks in our industry.

My rage drained away by the second, leaving just emptiness and guilt.

Jenny was the last one on the couch. She sat there in silence, eyeing me. "Are you okay?"

"I will be. I'm just a mess now."

She offered me a hug, and I took it.

Jenny stood up, straightening her workout shorts. "Just focus on Bret. Everything will work out." Then she walked right past me, following the rest of the girls into the studio behind her.

A director inside the studio clapped her hands sharply twice, then hollered, "Chop, chop, people. The dance waits for no woman."

Vika shouldn't have found out like this. I had wanted to tell her but didn't get the chance before the gossip sites leaked my new relationship.

I walked over to the couch and dropped onto it, more exhausted than I'd been recently. My ballroom career was over, even if we did win Blackpool. And now I'd probably be on the cover of *Star* magazine.

Because I chose to be with Bret.

I loved him—and he loved me too.

But I had to tell him the truth about what happened with Dima and me years ago.

"Selena—now!" the director yelled. The beat of a techno tango ripped through the speakers. In a few minutes, I'd have to smile for the camera like life was just a peach. A happy, joy-joy, this-is-so-amazingly-fun peach.

*B*ack in Marin, Selena and I had settled into a nice daily routine. She moved into the houseboat. We'd hiked Mt. Tamalpais, camped at Angel Island, and spent the weekend at Xavier and Robyn's beach cottage in Bolinas. Life was idyllic away from the paparazzi in Los Angeles.

But we needed to have a talk about the future.

I took her out to dinner at Sushi Ran. We sipped sake and dined on the freshest sashimi I had ever had.

I gazed at her over the small table, enamored with my girl. "Let's talk, Sel. How are we going to make this work?"

Selena took a long sip of her glass of water. "Well—you are stationed at Camp Pendleton, which is only two hours from Los Angeles. We can live off base in Orange County. Maybe Laguna Nigel? Or Ladera Ranch? I have a friend who owns a dance studio down there so I can still teach. My students will come to me. And I can commute during the tapings." She paused. "I mean, after Blackpool, of course. I still need to be close to Dima until we compete."

I pursed my lips and nodded. I had accepted that she was going to still train with Dima until Blackpool, so I wasn't going to complain. She deserved to achieve her dream.

I was impressed that she'd at least already thought out some logistics of how we could stay together.

"Ladera Ranch or Laguna Nigel? Yah, I mean the locations are great because they're both close to the back gate of Pendleton, and I work right there. But those places are expensive. My housing allowance with dependents would be two thousand a month. So that could maybe work when we get married."

Selena spat out her water. "Married? Was that your version of some proposal? And don't worry about the housing prices, I can handle them."

My lips burned, and it wasn't from the wasabi. "No, Selena, when I propose, you'll know it. And it sure as hell won't be in a crowded restaurant. But let's cut the crap. Marriage is where this is heading, right? You didn't just ruin your dancing career to have a fling with me, did you? We've said I love you. You want kids and a family. I didn't just pick you up the other night at a bar. We have a past. And hopefully, a future. Plus, I'm a Marine. If we aren't married, you won't get any benefits."

Selena's chopsticks pushed around the fish on her plate. "Sorry, Bret, I didn't mean that. I'm just so overwhelmed. Please forgive me. Of course, I'd love to eventually get married and start a life with you. I'm just really worried about the tabloids. They're already having a field day with this story. They'll paint me as a vixen in some weird twisted love triangle." She paused, and her lips parted. She shook her head as if she changed her mind about what she was going to say. "Who knows what other lies they'll make up?"

What had she wanted to say? Was she hiding something? I kept my concerns to myself.

Selena continued. "It will be awful. I just know it. And I don't want to scare you away."

She was right—everything she said. What had I been thinking? Being on the show was one thing. I'd agreed to do it for my friend. Being a tabloid kicking toy was another.

My mind raced. This could ruin my career. Would they interview my friends and family? Would they twist my motive for going on this show as a devious attempt to get Selena back?

"Bret, babe, we can make it through this. I can talk to my publicist. But we just have to plan it."

"I refuse to be made the laughingstock of the Marine Corps."

"You don't have to be."

"I'm not going to lie. We didn't do anything wrong, and I'm not embarrassed by you."

She squeezed my hand. "Perfect. I'll contact my publicist and see what our options are. We will probably have to give an interview. It'll be fine. Trust me."

I tossed a piece of hamachi into my mouth. She was in the public eye, I knew this.

"Fine, Sel. I'm in. Just tell me what to do."

I knocked back another sake bomb, but my gut twisted. I thought Selena would be thrilled to talk about the future, but she panicked. There was something she wasn't telling me. I had to find out what she was hiding.

The alarm clock on my phone went off at four a.m. Selena and I had another long day ahead of us. I wanted to get on the road by five to skip the Bay Area traffic and start our journey down to Los Angeles.

I turned my phone alarm off and noticed a missed call and a voicemail from Ray. He was probably just calling to tease me again about my outfit from the first week—I'd already been fielding insults from my buddies since the show aired last week.

"Lord, Nia just showed me an article online about your scandalous affair with Selena. By the way, you looked like a fruitcake in that getup. Give me a call when you get a chance."

What the hell?

I googled my name, something I never thought I'd do.

Headlines popped up, one after another. *Radar Online, People, Us Weekly*. I clicked through the articles. Each carried a version of a heartbroken Dima finding out about Selena and me. Some included pictures of Selena and I dancing on the show, one even had my boot camp picture. Nothing shocking.

But then something caught my eye.

"A source close to the situation said that Bret and Selena broke up as teens after Selena cheated on Bret with Dima at a dance competition."

I slammed the computer shut. It was a tabloid, so it was probably not true.

Even so, heat rose in my chest, and I had difficulty breathing. I always assumed that Dima had seduced her, but I was dumb enough to believe that it had been after Selena and I broke up.

But the thought that she had cheated on me had consumed me at the time.

I had been so lonely in boot camp—the thought of Dima touching Selena had tortured me. For years at night, I would picture them fucking, and it drove me insane, like a never-ending porno in my mind.

But to read it in the press made it more painful. Now I was just another reality loser that the tabloids could use to sell magazines. I looked over at Selena, still sound asleep. It was probably better that she wasn't awake yet. I would try to calm down.

I attempted to take my mind off the rumors by reading the morning paper that had been slipped under the door.

An hour later, Selena rolled over, her tank top scrunched on her stomach. "Morning. Did I oversleep?"

"Forget that, Selena. I have to show you something." I clicked on the website.

She sat up, brushed her hair out of her eyes, and focused on the screen.

I studied her eyes. She skimmed the page, until she gasped for breath—then bit her lip.

It was true.

"Look me in the eye, and don't lie to me. What happened?" I could tell her mind was racing, trying to think of what to say to me.

Selena blinked furiously. "Bret, I ...I wanted to tell you so many times—"

I slammed my fist into the bed. "Are you kidding me, Sel? You *wanted to tell me that you cheated on me?* And now I find out the details from the tabloids?"

"Bret, please! I was so young!"

"Do you have any idea how tough it was for me to get over you? I joined the Corps to make a good life for *you*—for us! We agreed that we wanted to be on our own, not dependent on our parents. I had no money or education. The military was the only way—there was no money in ballroom back then for amateurs, and it would've taken us years and a ton of money to turn pro. Plus, you know I never really enjoyed it. I only danced because my parents forced me, and then when I got paired with you, I just wanted to make you happy. In boot camp, every time I got trashed on the quarterdeck, doing pushups 'til my fingers bled, I got through it because I knew I was doing it for our future. And then you left me—and you didn't even have the decency to show up at my graduation to tell me to my face."

Selena's chin quivered. "I had no idea how hard it was for you, Bret. I have nothing to say for myself. I was just so devastated and confused."

"What happened? That competition was only a few weeks after I left. The truth. You didn't even wait that long. You owe me the truth."

She grit her teeth. "Well, Dima convinced me to do a Pro/Am competition. Since it was in Miami, we shared a hotel room. I had no money, so Dima paid for everything. My flight. The entry fees. Even bought me a new dress."

"Oh, isn't he generous."

"After the competition, we went back to our room. And to celebrate, he ordered champagne and strawberries."

It took me a second to register what she was saying. "Wait, he got you drunk?"

"Well, that's not really his fault. I mean, he ordered the champagne. But I willingly drank it."

"But you were eighteen, Selena. He was twenty-eight."

"So you never drank underage Bret? Don't be a hypocrite."

"That's not the point. How drunk did you get?"

She pursed her lips. "Drunk. I don't remember what happened. But I woke up in Dima's bed. Naked. Dima told me that we had slept together. I was so ashamed Bret. I knew that you would never forgive me, so I ended it between us."

What in the fuck? The room seemed to be spinning as I tried to process this information.

This was even worse than being cheated on. Did she even realize she had been raped? I had imagined this scenario a thousand different ways, but I never ever thought that I'd lost her because Dima had raped her.

I needed to tread lightly. I was no longer angry at her. But she needed to understand what had happened.

"Selena. Listen to me. He raped you."

She shook her head. "No, not at all. It was nothing like that. I was in the room with him alone. I traveled with him. I drank."

"None of that matters. Even if you hadn't had a fiancé, he raped you. This is not your fault."

Her hand shook. "No. It is my fault. Dima would never—"

"Why are you defending him? He got you drunk and then took advantage of you. He destroyed us. Don't you see Selena? The tabloids are wrong. You didn't cheat on me. You were raped."

"He said I wanted it. That I came on to him."

Jesus. "Of course, he did. That motherfucker. Why didn't you tell me? I wouldn't have been mad at you. I loved you."

"I wanted to write you so many times, but Dima said—"

"Dima?!"

Selena slumped on the bed. "I planned to tell you. But you were away for three months, and the guilt grew. I didn't think you would ever want me. I was so ugly and fat. After that happened, I was so depressed that I just gorged myself on food. I was so alone. But then Dima came to see me. Told me he could make me over. He put me on a diet plan and trained me. Then he asked me to dance with him. I couldn't say no. I thought you would never want me again after what I did."

Fuck. This was even worse. "He did that all on purpose, Sel. He always teased you about your weight and your acne, no matter how many times I told him to shut the fuck up. He tore you down so he could transform you into a swan. His swan."

Her hands shook. "Maybe he did. But I was so lost. So, I chose to dance with Dima. I'm sorry I didn't come to your graduation, but I didn't think I could handle seeing you knowing what I had done. It was cowardly. Once I gained some perspective, I tried to find you. But you had vanished. Ever since then, I've looked for you. Facebook, Instagram. But you were gone. Completely gone. It's like you existed only in my memories. You don't know the guilt I've felt. I've wanted to tell you since we got back together, and I tried to, but you didn't want to talk about the past. I screwed up. I don't know what to say other than I'm sorry. Please forgive me, Bret."

I could forgive her. She hadn't done anything wrong.

But I could never forgive Dima. I was going to beat the shit out of him next time I saw him.

"You don't need to ask my forgiveness because you did nothing wrong. But you can't dance with Dima anymore."

Her mouth twisted. "You can't tell me what I can do. Of course, I'm going to dance with Dima. We have one more competition left. The competition. I can't just walk away."

"He's a rapist. I can't trust him. He could do it again. You should press charges."

"It was ten years ago! And I don't remember what happened. Maybe I did come on to him?"

"You were drunk, Sel. And a kid."

"It's just one more competition."

"Yeah. One more competition. You have a bunch of titles. You don't need this one. Not with your rapist."

"You are being irrational. It's in the past. He won't touch me."

"You don't know that. And you don't know that he won't do that to someone else. Like Elizabeth. I was supportive of you doing one more comp, but not anymore."

Selena broke into sobs. "Please Bret...please!"

"I'm done, Selena." I didn't turn around. I put on my shirt and shoes, leashed up Banjo, grabbed my bags, then slammed the door behind me.

After I made my way on the dock, I got into my truck and just drove.

Selena could fly to Los Angeles.

This was it for me. No more women. I'd gone against my better judgment getting involved with Selena again. I had been happier with no complications, just my loyal dog and my buddies. Buddies who would die for me. My brothers in the Corps were the only people I trusted.

I thought about Robyn's words to me recently about my path. I didn't believe her mumbo jumbo for a second, but she was right about one thing: had I never done this show, I never would have reunited with Selena, nor would I have found out about what had happened with Dima.

My heart ached at the loss...but also, I felt strangely at peace. For the first time since Selena had left me years ago, I knew that I'd finally found the complete closure I'd always craved.

I cried myself back to sleep after Bret left. I called and texted him repeatedly, but my calls went straight to voicemail, and my texts went unanswered. He had already written me off.

Not that I could blame him. I had created this mess, so many years ago. Ever since our reunion, I'd tried to tell him, but he didn't want to talk about it.

I was sure it was Dima who'd told the tabloids that I cheated. I knew Dima was angry, but that would be really low—even for him.

But though Dima had always convinced me that I was the one who cheated, now I was wondering if Bret was right.

Did Dima really rape me? In my mind, there was a big difference between rape and being taken advantage of, but the lines were blurry now.

At least I had no more secrets. I hoped and prayed that Bret would calm down and take me back. But I knew Bret. And that didn't seem likely.

Clearly I was a mess.

And I needed to see a therapist and figure out how to process what happened with Dima.

When I'd composed myself enough, I called Benny and explained that I wouldn't be able to go to Los Angeles today. I would take the day off. The thought of sitting for hours in an airport and then on a plane with nothing to do but stew about Bret sounded like agony. I could at least put off the flight until later that night.

But tomorrow, I would have to see Bret.

We had a group hip-hop dance practice.

THE NEXT DAY

Benny's eyes lit up the minute he caught me bouncing through Brooks Ballroom studio modeling the new line of *Dancing Under the Stars* women's hip-hop dancewear. He twirled me around, and we danced a few steps of the quickstep he had choreographed for Xavier and me.

I smiled and broke into some crunking moves. Benny had made me the official choreographer for the dance. That was the good news. The bad news was that I'd have to spend seven hours in the same room as Bret and Dima.

I knew this studio was Vika's turf, but I took a cab straight from the airport super early to help the set designers give it a street vibe. I hung up some paper on the walls and got some hip-hop dancer friends of mine to spray paint urban graffiti, swapped out the blue velvet curtains for some black rayon ones, and hired a DJ to set up a real booth. The cameramen and sound guys were milling around the room after they hooked up the LCD flat-screen television I'd requested. Benny had brought in the newest designs for everyone to try on, and the crew even set up some strobe lights. I hoped everyone could feel the vibe.

Bret had arrived ten minutes ago but had gone straight to the back of the studio. He didn't even look at me. My heart ached.

The other dancers started piling into the studio, two by two as if getting ready for a trip on an ark. As soon as they walked into the studio, the costume girl handed them workout wear to put on. But Eric and Nicole, who usually arrived at the studio arm in arm, carting matching Starbucks lattes, headed to opposite corners of the studio. Nicole looked pale, and her usual shellacked ponytail was askew.

Had Nicole found out about Eric being with another guy? Ugh, I hope she was okay.

"Alright, people!" I clapped my hands. This ball was mine, and I ran with it. "Let's do this. We've got some hip-hopping to do."

I walked over to the music booth and told the DJ what to play. "Is everyone here?"

"Dima isn't here yet," Vika said, her eyes glued to the door.

"He's not?" I hadn't even noticed his absence. I looked at the clock. It was nearly nine o'clock. Was he now avoiding me?

"I texted to him," Vika mumbled, "but haven't heard back."

"Well, I'm sure he'll show up." I gave Vika a reassuring smile, but she looked stressed. Time to distract. "I'm so excited about this group hip-hop thing. I love urban dance, and I've been experimenting with some crunking and breaking, so this is gonna be off the hook." I glanced around the room. The cameramen were setting up. Benny kissed Vika goodbye. Vika gave me the evil eye when she saw me watching, and on the opposite side of the room, Bret paced around the floor.

"So," I started, "we have to do an eight-count as a group in the beginning, and then the partners each do a breakout solo. The order for the solos is Bret, Jenny, Jared, Vika, Ricardo, Elizabeth, Eric, Nicole, Dima, and I will close. I'll work on all your solos later, but let's get started on the group part. We're dancing to one of my favorite songs, Rob Base and DJ E-Z Rock's "Joy and Pain." But let's begin with a warmup. It's old school to get you in the mood."

I signaled the sound guy. He flipped on the strobe lights then started playing Cameo's "Word Up." I loved that song. Reminded me of high school jazz class, since my instructor had been stuck in the eighties.

I skipped to the front of the room and led everyone in a dance isolation routine. "Roll your hips to the right, now to the left, now circles." The lights were kicking on and off, and Bret kept making goofy faces into the mirror as he tried to keep up with me. Hip-hop wasn't his thing but he was doing a pretty good job.

"That's it, Bret! Bend your knees. Good!" He ignored me, but Vika was actually following her steps and not giving me any attitude. And I hated to admit it, but she looked super cute in her low-rise pink hip-hop pants and matching bra tank top, which her breasts filled out perfectly.

Two hours into the actual choreography, Dima strolled in like he was in no rush, and the DJ cut the sound. Dima would get away with it, though. None of us were stupid enough to question him.

"Dude, where've you been?" Bret asked.

Well, almost none of us.

"None of your business," Dima barked. "I'm here now."

"Hell yeah, it's my business." Bret got right up in his face, sweating and huffing from the routine. "We've all been here for two whole hours, and now we're gonna have to be here even longer to catch your ass up."

Dima pushed Bret's shoulder.

Dima must've had a death wish.

The other dancers froze in position as stocky six-feet, two-hundred-thirty-pound Bret looked at a gangly six-feet-two-inch and a buck-sixty Dima.

I cringed—this wasn't gonna be good.

Bret narrowed his eyes, and his voice deepened. "Back up, Dima. You don't want to fight me."

"Don't tell to me what to do!" Dima cursed in Russian and flew at Bret.

But Bret threw Dima down and had him in a headlock faster than I could say cha-cha. Dima's scrawny legs were kicking in the air like a psycho Popeye cartoon. It would almost be funny if I wasn't sure Dima was about to die.

"You motherfucker. You fucking raped her!"

Oh my God!

"*Dimichka! Dimichka!*" Vika screamed. "Somebody do something!"

Eric, Ricardo, and Jared were on it. They dove in and yanked Dima and Bret apart, successfully ending the combat. Then, after only a second of peace, Dima sucker-punched Bret.

Bret roundhouse kicked him in the face, and blood gushed from Dima's nose.

The referees broke it up again. Like two snarling dogs, Dima and Bret had to be pulled to opposite sides of the room.

This was crazy. And it was all my fault.

I always loved the drive to Bolinas. It was windy and beautiful—the perfect escape from Hollywood and Selena.

The producers had the idea of filming my practice session with Robyn on the beach, which was fine by me. Bolinas was a great town. Selena used to want to own a little cottage on the beach here and spend her days playing with our kids in the sand. An ideal artist community, Bolinas was the home to surfers, poets, writers, artists, and recluses.

In order to keep their little slice of paradise hidden, the locals always destroyed any signs that identified the town. Robyn and I made the journey without needing a map, but I was delighted when we lost the filming crew behind us. I figured they would head farther down Highway One before they realized they'd missed the unmarked turn.

Robyn pointed ahead. "Could you stop here?"

I pulled in front of the Coast Café. We ran inside and ordered two coffees. I loved the surfboards that were hanging from the ceiling.

Robyn seemed mesmerized by the quaint town. We looked at the locals down below on the courtyard from the café's sunny deck.

I took a sip of my coffee. "I feel like I'm back in the seventies."

"Yeah, isn't it awesome?" Robyn blended into the local scene.

My mind drifted to Selena. We had spent our last weekend together here before the cheating story leaked. Selena had even mentioned that she wanted to get married on the beach.

Robyn put her hand on my shoulder. "I can see you're struggling with something."

"There's nothing to say. Selena and I gave our relationship another try, and it didn't work out. End of story."

"This isn't about that, is it? This is about her cheating. I read the article."

I grimaced.

"Look, Bret. Selena was young. I'm not saying what she did was okay, but it was her path."

Bret wasn't in the mood to listen to her New Age dogma. "It wasn't the cheating. I think she was raped, which, of course, is not her fault. But she doesn't see it that way and still wants to compete at Blackpool with Dima. I can't accept that."

"I will never ever condone an assault, but that is for her to figure out, not you. Don't you see, Bret? This was your journey. To help her heal. She needs you. We don't have to share the same beliefs, but you can't live in the past. You must be present, be here now."

"I never thought of it that way." I had been so angry with Selena for still wanting to dance with him after she should realize what he did to her.

"You know, things haven't always been perfect with Xavier and me. In the earlier years, I found out that he had cheated on me when he was on the road. I was devastated—filled with so much rage. I blamed him, myself, his music. I left him and filed for divorce. It ended up being a good time for me, though. I focused on improving myself—I learned how to meditate, studied yoga, took a painting class. Once I released all the anger I had toward Xavi, I realized that no matter what, I still loved him. I am happier with him, despite his betrayal than I am on my own. He had learned from his mistakes also, and now we are stronger than ever. So, what I'm saying is that if Selena makes you happy, and you truly love her, you owe it to yourself to forgive her...or you'll never be at peace."

The cool ocean breeze made me shiver. "I still don't see how we could ever create a life together. We're just too different."

"Yes, you are different. But she loves you, I can see that. And sometimes, that is enough."

We finished our coffees and headed into town. The shoot was on "The Patch"—a gorgeous stretch of sand that was popular for longboarders. A group of photographers stood under a makeup canopy, with production people huddled behind them. I was sure the locals were not thrilled with the shoot littering their beloved beach with cameras, dressing trailers, and stylists.

As I sat in the makeup chair for my on-location clip, I scanned the scenery for Selena, just in case she popped up with Xavier. She had a habit of showing up everywhere I was. She wasn't here, which was a relief.

But no matter how hard I tried to push her out of my mind, she kept haunting my thoughts.

SELENA

It had been weeks since Dima and Bret's fight. I still hadn't spoken to Bret. At least I would have fun tonight—Xavier was throwing a huge bash. Bret would never come, though. He hated parties and costumes.

But first, I had to focus on the show.

"Ladies and Gentlemen, put your hands together for Xavier and Selena, who will be dancing a swing to the Ray Charles classic 'Hit the Road Jack.'"

Xavier and I glided onto the stage. He looked so fine in his Pachuco-Zoot-Suit-inspired digs. The man had gotten into the creation of his costume, big time. He'd called all of his fashion gurus in to design the perfectly authentic outfit: a black and red pinstriped double-breasted jacket with sleeves that hung to the end of his fingertips, a cardinal-tinted silk shirt, flowing pegged pants, a black fedora with a scarlet feather, a long wallet chain and tan *calcos* shoes with squared-off bulldog toes. Classic.

And they'd hooked me up, too: a killer red plumed skirt with a black ruby-bedazzled corset studded with diamonds and rubies, and a huge red-feathered head-dress. I'd even stuck a switchblade knife into my bouf-fant-styled hair. H-O-T, baby.

The audience went wild when we began to dance. Swing was one of my best dances, and for tonight, I had choreographed a very Lindy Hop-inspired routine. The two of us flicked up our heels in unison and flew across the floor.

Xavier was divine. A true musician. He pulled out all the stops. He had even planned a huge Zoot Suit bash.

We did our signature sugar push move, with Xavier tossing me away then yanking me back, and I knew we had nailed this number. As we kicked into our final pose, the music came to a crashing end and applause exploded from the audience. Boo-yah, baby!

Both of us breathing heavily, we headed over to Matt. It was pretty stupid trying to interview dancers in the seconds after a performance, but that was *Dancing Under the Stars*, so there we were, two panting dogs dressed to the nines.

"So, Xavier," host Matt said, "you look quite dapper tonight. Audience, doesn't he look dapper?"

"Come on, people, show me some love!" Xavier shouted. They did, of course. Loudly. "*Oye, ese*, I gotta tell ya. This crowd is amazing. Give it up for my *guisa* Selena! Yeah! Show some love. She is bangin'. Those moves are *hot*. I mean, this dance is very special to me, very special to me, for real. I'm Chicano, and *mi abeulo* was a *Pachuco*. In preparation for this dance, I studied the richness and culture during World War II, back in the 1940s. How Mexican-Americans had an integral part in creating the music and dancing swing. In fact, in honor of what I have learned from this dance, I'm gonna create a special Zoot-Suit-inspired line of clothing for my line, *Xavier Tomás* Clothing." Xavier pounded his fist over his heart. "I feel it, Matt. I feel it deep."

"Xavier, that's great. It's wonderful that you've taken such an interest in the history of ballroom dance.

Selena, what do you think about Xavier's newfound inspiration?"

"Well, I don't know much about history," I mumbled. "But Xavier's the best. He's so great and supportive of me, and I love his outfit." Yeah, that would go down in the archives as the best answer ever. I hated doing interviews; I just wanted to dance.

"Let's see what the judges had to say. Benjamin Brooks?"

"Xavier, my good bastard, that was a beaut'. Love your duds. You got the style of the dance down," Benny said.

"Karen Lopez," Matt said

"Xavier, you are a dream. You gave such an authentic feel to the dance. I can see that you made a strong effort to include some Lindy Hop moves into your swing, but I really appreciate the fact that you still danced with traditional timing," she said.

"Steve Samson," Matt asked.

"Xavier, you're like a rocket. Taking off fast and furious. It was superb," Steve replied.

"After the break, the judges will reveal their scores," said Matt.

Xavier and I headed backstage. We awaited our scores surrounded by the other dancers. The judges gave us three tens!

Thank God, we were the last dance of the night. Xavier and I plowed through the after-show press junket as fast as we could. I rushed to my trailer to change. Jenny and Elizabeth were already inside waiting for me so we could go together.

Jenny leaned over my sink, scrubbing off her makeup. Water beads trickled down her forehead. "There you are. Can you please tell Queen Elizabeth over here that what she's wearing is underwear and not an actual dress?" Jenny grabbed a towel and wiped off her face.

Elizabeth pranced around in a near see-through pink silk slip. "It is *too* a dress," she whined. "It's a Diane von Furstenberg. Vika let me borrow it." She twirled around like a princess.

Apparently, Jenny and I weren't as cool as Vika. Elizabeth had ditched us last week to attend store grand openings with Vika and Nicole.

Jenny whipped the towel at Elizabeth. "Elizabeth, please stop taking fashion advice from Vika. She was a stripper."

Elizabeth pouted. "No, she wasn't. She was a go-go dancer. It's not the same thing."

Just one day of peace is all I ask. "Come on, guys. Jenny, stop giving her such a hard time about everything. What do you want her to wear? Braids and a cotton ankle-length dress?"

Jenny slipped into a navy knee-length skirt.

I backed up to Elizabeth, who unhooked my corset.

Ahh, to breathe again.

"Jen, you did so much better tonight. Dion even stood up straight."

Jenny zipped up her boots. "Yes, Dion's improving rapidly. But I think overall, he's better at the Standard dances."

I threw on my favorite dress and fastened my five-inch pumps. "This party is gonna be awesome. Come on. Let's go."

Xavier's customized *carucha* waited outside to take us to the jamboree.

Would Bret show up?

Xavier outdid himself this time. He had hired a celebrity event designer to coordinate his "Zoot Suit Bash." Xavier rented out the ballroom of the Beverly Hills L'Hermitage hotel and booked the Los Angeles Philharmonic Orchestra for a night of 1940s-era swing jazz music. It would be off the scale, this shindig. Party of the century, if not the millennium.

We entered through an elegant lobby, crowned by a majestic crystal chandelier, then climbed two flights of marble steps. With each step, the sounds of the orchestra grew louder, and then we arrived, and the doors burst open.

It was even better than I had imagined: the raised bandstand filled with gleaming instruments, the pulsating music, and the bubbly performers set against vibrant orange and blue decor. And the dance floor—God! I'd never seen anything like it. Burnished maple, accented by a shiny brass rail tracing its perimeter. There were round tables, and a soda fountain dispensing tall mugs of Mexican Coke for a nickel each.

It was gorgeous here. I thought I had died and landed on the set of the play *Zoot Suit*. I loved it.

Xavier took the stage as my posse and I moved through the crowd.

"*¿Que Pasiones?* Welcome, everybody, to the new Savoy Ballroom," he said into a microphone. "I have created this evening in appreciation for the jazz legends who inspired me: Tin-Tan, Cab Calloway, and Lalo Guerrero. Ladies and gentlemen, the music never stops at the Zoot Suit Bash. I also wanted to bring awareness to the Sleepy Lagoon murder trial and the Zoot Suit Riots. *Al rato, vato.*"

He waved his arm broadly to the left. The spotlight followed, picking up Latin music sensation Luis Sanchez emerging from the wings.

Can this night get any better?

Onstage, Luis, wearing a purple zoot suit, belted out Lalo Guerrero's song, "Los Chucos Suaves."

The girls and I walked up to the bar, and I ordered a margarita, some chips and guacamole, and a few taquitos.

"Hey, Sel," Bret said.

I turned to face him. He was also costumed in head-to-toe 1940s garb—and looking way sexy in the midnight-blue double-breasted zoot suit.

I couldn't even believe he was here!

"What are you doing here?" I said, stepping to the other side of him. "You hate parties."

"I do. But I wanted to see you." He ordered a shot of tequila. "You wanna dance? For old time's sake?"

Elizabeth gave me a huge grin. She mouthed, *He totally loves you,* and then led Jenny away from the bar.

I scanned the room. "I thought you were done with me."

"I was upset. I'm still upset." He took a deep breath and downed his tequila. He licked a drop from his lips —the lips that had kissed every inch of my body.

"Oh. Well, in that case, fine." I held up my plate. "But let me finish my food? I'm starving."

Bret laughed.

I took a big ol' bite of the taquito and a nibble of a chip smothered in guac and—*uh-oh.*

Benny had spotted me stuffing my face.

I tossed my plate behind a large plant and grabbed Bret's hand. "No time like the present."

Benny was still pushing through the crowd when Bret whisked me away to safety.

He led me to the packed floor. Luis sang another song. I dug into my purse and popped a mint into my mouth before tossing my bag onto a nearby table. Then I wrapped myself in Bret's arms. *Ummmm.* I couldn't believe I'd gone ten years without these arms.

He squeezed me tight. "Do you remember that time in Croatia at Junior Worlds when we ditched our sponsor and spent the entire night playing cards with that Icelandic guy, Ingibjörg?"

"Totally. And we still won the next day." I rested my head on his shoulder.

His hands lowered to my hips and he swayed me into him. "Selena... I'm sorry. I couldn't deal with the fact that Dima took advantage of you. And seeing my name in the tabloids...I just couldn't handle it." He pulled my chin up with his thumb and forced me to look at him. "You should've told me what happened.

You wanted me to join the Corps. I would've done anything for you."

"Bret, I was so emotional after that night. I didn't know what happened, so I blamed myself. After I had slept with him, I didn't think you would take me back."

"I would've killed him."

"Yeah, I saw the way you fought him."

"He groomed you, took advantage of you, it's not okay. He will do it to another girl."

"I know." And I did. I just didn't know what to do.

He spun me around to a drumroll. When I landed back in his arms, he squeezed me even tighter. "See that? You can spin away, but you always end up in my arms." He kissed my neck.

Good gawd, did this man remember my buttons?

"It feels so good to have you back in my arms," he said into my ear.

The saxophone kicked in, slowing the tempo even more. He twirled me around.

"I love you, Sel. I never stopped." He cradled my face and looked into my eyes. There he went, letting his emotions rocket to the moon—and taking me with him.

I had forgotten how good that ride could feel.

"I love you, too." I leaned into Bret, my first love. He embraced me in his arms, and I remembered who I had been when I'd started to dance with him. We'd built our world together. And I'd torn it apart.

And now I was back where I should be. In his embrace. Swaying to the music as if we had never been apart.

BRET

J peeked through the backstage curtains to look at the audience. The place was completely packed, including my parents, Ray and his family, Pierce's family, and my entire unit in the front row. The producers must've arranged it with the base.

I wanted to puke.

Twenty-one *million* people watched last week. Twenty-one million people had watched me gyrate half-naked. I'd even received two marriage proposals. They were from jail, but still.

Someone get me a bucket...

I jumped up and down and shook my head and arms to loosen up. Robyn grabbed my hands and gave me a kiss on the head.

"It's ours, babe. Don't you worry. Here, let's say a prayer."

"A prayer? You just said don't worry."

"Shut up and pray, boy." We bowed our heads and thanked the Lord for all our blessings. "Amen," Robyn said. "Okay, let's go show them how it's done. Boo-YA!" Robyn gave me a high-five.

A producer hustled into the room. "Everyone in the red room! We're on in five minutes," he said. Selena grabbed her ankle and stretched it. Vika propped her leg on the couch and leaned over into a split. Jenny took a big puff on her inhaler as the guys started barking and chest-bumping each other like a bunch of high school jocks. Behind us, Dima and his celebrity partner were kissing on the sofa. Robyn slapped Xavier playfully on the back of the head.

Selena grabbed her other ankle and leaned toward me. "We made it through the season. Can you believe we're in the finale together?"

I nodded, my eyes wide, and then finally exhaled. "No, I can't believe it. How I didn't get eliminated that first week, I'll never know. No, wait, I do know," I kissed her, "you helped me."

Jenny helped Selena get ready. "I can't believe we've been doing this show for five seasons. God help me, Sel, I actually *love* being on this show. Who would have thought it? And I'm glad you're back with Bret. You seem really happy."

Selena gave her a reluctant nod. "Thank you," she said. "Now stop messin' with my 'do and get outta my way, I got a crystal-encrusted dance shoe trophy to claim, be-yotch."

"We're on in three, two, one," the producer said.

Matt's voice boomed over the speakers. "In a season filled with triumph, scandal, and heartache... Now, the final three standing will prove to you why they should be the winners. Tonight, our finalists will come together for a Paso Doble Pow Wow, and the always exciting freestyle. Tomorrow, we will crown a new champion. Ten couples started, and only three remain. Live, it's the *Dancing Under the Stars* finale!"

We all walked out when the intro music started and took our places side by side on the stage, dressed in complementary black and red paso doble outfits. I waved at Pierce's family sitting in the front row. I knew that Pierce was smiling down on me.

The cast had to stand there while long clips rolled of each of us babbling about which were our favorite dances of the season. Robyn and I picked our opening night mambo and our Viennese waltz. I watched our clip of the Viennese. She looked so graceful, flying across the stage effortlessly. We skated around the floor as if we were walking on water. Tomorrow, the seven eliminated couples would all come back to dance for the finale, but tonight the producer filled up the airtime by torturing the audience with these videos.

By the time Dima and Laura and Xavier and Selena's clips aired, we had been onstage for forty-five minutes. We hadn't even set a toe on the dance floor.

"Dancing together in our first ever Paso Doble Pow Wow." Matt waved his arm with a flourish. "Our *finalists*."

The music ripped through my body. Selena stood onstage with Robyn on her left and Laura on her right.

The men started on our knees and rose in unison. We strutted toward the ladies. The partners swung each of the women around us before throwing them into splits.

Dima and Laura started their solo, and Robyn, Selena, Xavier, and I slipped offstage, where we watched them from behind a curtain. Laura gave it her all and paraded around Dima. His shoulders relaxed, and he dropped his head toward her, and they pranced around the stage. Her shiny blonde hair reflected off her red satin gown. Dima and Laura collapsed on the floor, arms wrapped around each other.

Their steps may have been perfect, but I thought they'd been too reserved and never lost control. They sprinted offstage.

Xavier and Selena started their solo. The mood was totally different—they were on fire. The passion between them was electric, and they moved in unison. Xavier tapped his feet like a matador, and Selena teased him with her dress. She looked so sexy. Totally playing the moment, Xavier swaggered around Selena and then gave in, lowering to his knees. But even there, he stayed in charge. Clutching her waist, he rolled her into his arms.

Good job—but I knew the audience hadn't seen anything yet.

Robyn and I rushed onstage and stood alone on the floor. Two beats into our solo music, I thrashed my cape around, my chest erect. Robyn arched her back in defiance. The music started cascading as I beckoned her to me. Robyn twirled into my arms, and I seized her as the music exploded to full beat. We charged across the floor, bodies perfectly in sync. I felt like I was in a real bullfight, with my eye on the prize.

Dima and Laura had been flawless, Xavier and Selena had been passionate, but Robyn and I were fierce competitors, and we attacked the floor. The bass vibrated through my body, and I threw Robyn into a death drop. Spinning around, she landed perfectly on her toes.

This was my dance, my night, my mission. And I was alive.

The audience gave us a standing ovation. The camera panned to my Marines, who were clapping and catcalling me. Ray held a big sign that said, "Vote for Staff Sergeant Peacock." That bastard.

"Now what did the judges think?" Matt said. "Benjamin Brooks?"

Benny eyed Selena's outfit like he was scouting out a backup, just in case it didn't work with Vika.

Think again, old man. She's taken.

"Definitely the best paso doble we've ever seen on this show. Dima and Laura—of all the Latin dances, this is where you shined. Your height gave you both a strong presence. Xavier, your feet dragged across the floor, but your posture was strong. And Bret and Robyn— bugger me dead! *That* was bloody amazing! You're the team to beat."

I picked Robyn up and swung her around. I couldn't believe this was happening.

The other judges basically repeated what Benny said. Even though it was a group dance, we were judged individually because of our solos. Parading through the red room one couple at a time, Dima and Laura scored straight eights, and Xavier and Selena got two nines and an eight from Benny.

It was finally our turn, so Robyn and I headed into the red room, which the other dancers had already vacated.

Matt interviewed us. "Bret, how does it feel to be in the final on your first season of *Dancing Under the Stars?*"

I looked right into the camera and smiled. "Well, it's such a blessing to have made the final in my first and *only* season. And I've met the most wonderful people on this show. Robyn has been such an inspiration. She's a brilliant performer, and so successful."

"That's wonderful. And the scores for Bret and Robyn?"

I held my breath.

"Ten," Benny said.

Karen jumped out of her seat. "Ten!"

Steve held up the number. "Ten."

"A perfect thirty, and in the finale!" Matt said. He stuck the microphone in front of Robyn. "How do you feel?"

"I owe it all to Bret. He's the hardest-working dancer here, or anywhere. And he is an amazing man." Robyn winked at me.

"And Bret, any final thoughts?"

Could somebody pinch me? I can't believe that twenty-one million people all have tuned in to see me. I finally understood why everyone loved this show. And now *I* loved this show. My life had changed forever. "All I can say, Matt, is that this is the happiest night of my life."

Selena popped her head around the corner and shook it slowly, my girl's smile was better than any trophy could ever be. *I love you*, she mouthed at me.

I loved her too. And I planned to make her mine forever.

And even more shocking, I think I loved dancing.

"Welcome back to the live finale of *Dancing Under the Stars*. You saw the final three couples battle it out last night. And right now, one of our three finalists is about to be eliminated. Last night, millions of you voted online, called, and texted your votes," Matt said. "With those votes, combined with our judges' scores, we can now reveal which of our couples will be the first to be eliminated tonight."

Xavier had his arms around me onstage. Tonight was much tenser than last night's group-dance orgy. No chest-bumping backstage tonight. None of us were ready to fly the white flag now. Bret barely slept last night—I knew, because he kept me awake the whole time, tossing and turning. And I had fretted because I just wanted him to win.

The ominous elimination music began to play. "Xavier," Matt said, "last night, Karen said your freestyle was the most creative she's ever seen, but did the viewers agree?"

Our freestyle had been amazing. I had strung a medley of Xavier's greatest hits together, and we'd danced this cha-cha, rock-fusion number. Xavier had flipped me over like a tortilla.

"Laura, last night, Steve said your Viennese waltz was exquisite, but did the viewers think it was enough for you to win the trophy?"

Dima held Laura, who, despite the layers of tanning cream, looked very flush. They were out for sure. Her Latin actually really improved this season, but it was her Standard that landed her in the finale. Their Viennese waltz was exquisite—perfect lines, feet, and body posture. And she looked great during the paso doble. But it was her freestyle that killed their chances. She tried to dance a tango/cha-cha combo that just didn't flow well at all.

"And Robyn, Benny said you're the team to beat, and you received a perfect 30. But will the viewers send you to the finish line?"

Bret and Robyn looked confident and weren't even breaking a sweat with the hot lights shining in their faces. Her paso had been perfect. But in her freestyle, she went 100% hip-hop, and sometimes the viewers vote against that. But it didn't seem to faze Robyn. I studied Bret. It was nice to see him smile again. He seemed as happy as he had been when we were teens.

"The couple in third place is..." Matt paused, and the drum rolled. "Dima and Laura."

Yes, yes, yes! Xavier and I were in the final two!

Xavier threw his arms around me, and I swore I was going to suffocate. When he pulled back, I saw that I'd gotten glitter all over his white shirt.

"Look pro, Xavier," I whispered.

The audience gave Dima and Laura a standing ovation as they walked down the stairs from the stage. Matt embraced them. "Laura, you've gone from a teen mom to a dancer. Tell us what this experience has been like for you."

Dima clutched Laura to his chest. "It's been incredible. I met so many great people and learned so much about myself. But the best part of this entire experience has been meeting Dima. He's changed my outlook on my life, and he's a truly beautiful person inside and out."

Dima gave her a kiss on the mouth. I couldn't believe he would be so open about hooking up with his celebrity partner, especially since she was a teenager.

Bret was right. Dima was a creep.

Matt aborted the interview. "Ladies and gentlemen, Dima Volkov and Laura Benson. Coming up, a musical performance from John Matthew."

We headed back to the red room to watch John's performance. I couldn't believe the producers had convinced him to come on the show. Between Xavier, Bret, and John, I swore I'd been sucked right into some kind of childhood flashback.

Dima and Vika were huddled in the corner consoling Laura. I sat next to Bret.

Bret had to win this. I had won twice before—once with a boy-bander and once with an NHL hockey player. Bret needed to win now for Pierce's family. For himself.

"You nervous?" Bret asked. He was decked out in a tuxedo with tails. Like a prince.

"For once, I am. I just want you to win." John started singing my favorite song, "Careless Kiss." I closed my eyes and relaxed into Bret's arms. He kissed my neck, and I wanted to savor the moment forever. I loved Bret. He made me happy. And I deserved to be happy.

The song ended, and the producer called us back onstage.

"Here we go," Xavier said, pulling me up. He jutted out his elbow, ready to escort me like a proper gentleman. I slipped my hand through, and we walked down the long white hallway, right to where John was stepping off the stage. I couldn't help it—suddenly I was fourteen years old again. John was my dream long before Xavier's poster went up in my bedroom. I didn't even care that John was gay; my knees actually went weak standing so close to him.

"Good luck, love," John said, touching my arm.

I'd just touched John Matthew...while holding Xavier's hand! *Could life get any more fabulous?*

We took our place onstage. Bret and Robyn stood next to us, and I rushed over and hugged Robyn. Then Bret and Xavier jumped in, and we all hugged each other. It probably looked so hokey, but that was just how it was tonight. I swirled in emotions. Looking over at the audience, I saw I wasn't the only one. Bret's Marines were sitting next to Xavier and Robyn's kids, everyone looking so proud. Xavier's whole band had shown up also.

The place was packed tonight, standing-room only. I knew on television the ballroom looked huge, but there were only about four hundred people stuffed into the crowded soundstage. The cameras panned overhead to create the illusion of a sea of people. I didn't have to see the millions of viewers at home to feel their eyes on me. This finale wasn't like any of the others. This one, I really cared about.

"Good luck, Selena," Robyn told me.

I took her hand. "You, too." Robyn gave me a hesitant smile and squeezed my hand as we all four lined up for the final announcement.

The music came on. Matt took his position. "For the past fifteen weeks, these couples have lived in the studio and endured endless hours of practice and blisters on their feet. Right now, we will finally reveal the winner of this season of *Dancing Under the Stars*." He smiled so big, I swore his bleached teeth actually twinkled from the bright lights. "The winner of the crystal dance shoe trophy is..."

I looked over at the judges' table. Benny was grinning at Bret. He mouthed, *You did it!*

I bit my lip.

Matt read the card. "Robyn Quintana and Bret Lord!"

My screams were drowned out by the howls of the audience as Bret lifted Robyn and twirled her around in the air. He did it! All the dancers and stars from the season flooded the stage. Xavier embraced his wife as confetti hailed the stage.

Bret looked me in the eye and kissed me on the lips, the camera inches from our faces.

Ten years later, Bret Lord had won another dance competition.

Then he dropped to his knees and pulled a ring box out of his pocket.

Oh my god!

"Selena, will you marry me?"

I sat in front of the television in Kuwait, my Marines around me. The familiar theme song blasted through the speakers.

"Come on, man, do we have to watch this crap? The fight is on," a corporal yelled.

My eyes remained glued to the screen. "I'll switch in a few. This is the only way I can see my wife."

"Welcome to *Dancing Under the Stars*. This season, we'll thrill with our best lineup ever, including a heavy metal drummer, an Olympic figure skater, and an Academy-Award-winning actor. But first, a showcase of our professionals," the host said.

The ladies hit the stage. Not much had changed—Vika, Nicole, Elizabeth, and Jenny were still there. There was a new girl also, some knockout with long, black hair.

Ray leaned toward me. "I knew you would come back to your senses and get out of the Corps. You will be back on that stage in a year."

"It's crazy. I can't believe it myself. I got more than I ever wanted."

Had I ever. My total prize money with endorsements had equaled $250,000. I had donated it all to Pierce's family. Pierce's wife, Kimberly, had initially refused to accept the money. She eventually gave in and used it to purchase a home and set up college funds for her children.

The only item I kept from the show was my truck. And I made peace with that decision.

"That samba was choreographed by former *Dancing Under the Stars* champion, Selena Lord."

The camera panned to Selena, who sat in the audience. She looked beautiful. Her hair was now dark, and she was dressed in a mint-colored wrap dress that showed off her tiny baby bump. She blew a kiss to the camera, and I knew that it was meant for me.

We'd had a small wedding ceremony on the beach in Bolinas, with just our families, Pierce's family, Jenny, Ray and his family, and Xavier and Robyn in attendance. After a one-week honeymoon to Lana'i, we'd returned to Camp Pendleton.

Selena had told Dima that she didn't want to compete in Blackpool with him. She also told him that she thought what had happened in that hotel room ten years ago was rape. Though she didn't press charges, she *did* tell Benny, who had Dima kicked off the show.

After our initial fight, I had not brought it up again. Selena had come to this decision on her own. And I was damn proud of her.

The irony of it all was now Dima's career in the dance world was over. And Selena's was just beginning.

Selena kept her Hollywood Hills home, and we'd also taken married housing on base. Now Selena taught at a local dance studio, even as she choreographed Xavier's new tour and this new season of *Dancing Under the Stars*.

A week before I had been deployed, we'd found out that Selena was pregnant. My deployment would only be five months, so I'd be back in time for the birth.

I rubbed my titanium wedding band. Though I wished I could be with her, I was happy to be serving alongside my men, even if it would be my final tour. Selena would be waiting for me when I returned, and I was going to be a father.

I had everything I'd ever wanted.

And so did Selena—I had agreed once my enlistment was up that I would compete with her. Sure, I wanted to make her happy, but I had also realized how much I loved dancing. So I was doing it for me as well.

I reached out and flipped the channel. "Enough samba for one day. Time for some UFC."

Thank you for reading The Swan and The Sergeant!

I hope you loved Bret & Selena.
Would you like to read a deleted bonus scene about
Bret & Selena?
Click here:

Catch up with them and meet their friends, Dax & Mirasol in The Angel & The Rockstar—A Navy SEAL Rumpelstiltskin Retelling!

Turn the page for an excerpt from
The Angel and The Rockstar

Or read about Bret's Marine buddy Grady who also falls in love with a ballroom dancer.
But without her love, I'm not a man—I'll remain forever a beast.
The Beauty and The Beast

Available now: Book 1 in the Heroes Ever After Series

ONE CLICK ***The Beauty and The Beast*** **now!**

XOXO
Alana

THE ANGEL & THE ROCKSTAR

DAX

J jerked back my head, flinging my blond hair off my face, the sweat dripping down my bare chest. My fingers remained glued to the strings, strumming the final riffs of our rock ballad. Ten thousand rabid fans mouthed the lyrics—the stadium glowed from the synchronized cigarette lighters, the night air pungent with drug fumes. A half naked girl surfed the crowd, minions throwing her on stage, as if they were offering a sacrifice, kneeling at the altar of their rock god—me. What an incredible night. I better fucking enjoy it—because tonight would be my last show, the last time I would make love to this guitar, the last time I would sing our songs. Tonight would be the night my chords would go silent.

But fuck it, tonight wasn't over yet. I was going to live it up. Fuck the finest woman in the audience, get completely wasted, maybe even trash a hotel room. My backstabbing band mates—guys I'd known since we were cub scouts—could go fuck themselves. I'd practiced in my parents' garage with these two-timing sons of bitches since before we reached puberty. We'd broken every barrier in the industry, brought heavy metal music back from obscurity, bridged the gap between rock star and celebrity.

I scanned the crowd, looking for my victim. Usual suspects milled in the crowd—bleached blonde bimbos, marked metal maidens, slutty sorority sisters. But for my last night as a rock star, I wanted someone innocent. Not a virgin, fuck no, I wanted some girl to ride me like a Harley. But I wanted a good girl, a girl who didn't sleep around, a girl who would never dare indulge in her rock star fantasy. A girl who would remember me forever.

What people didn't get about rockstars was that everything was handed to us. Yes men surrounded me, my every whim catered to. I wanted a challenge. For once in my life, I wanted to have to work for something.

My drummer Callan battled the bass drum, and my throat tightened. This was it. My final note. I plucked the last string, the sound soaring in my ears. A lump grew in my throat, and my eyes watered, but it wasn't from the smoke filled air. It was over. I clutched my beloved guitar, the instrument that had been my lifeline for so many years, and smashed it on the ground. Every bang, every slam, every crack filled me with rage. Chips of wood flew on the stage, strings popped, and I destroyed my prized possession. I glanced back at the audience, my heart pounding in my chest. I gave them a final wave goodbye, flicked off my traitorous bandmates, and exited stage left.

Publicists milled backstage, reporters shoved microphones in my face, and girls screamed when I walked by. Too easy. I wanted something real, a connection. Even though I would never be good for anything more than a one-night stand.

I grabbed a bottle of jack and took a swig; the smooth liquid coated my throat. I was hungry, but wasn't in the mood for the butter-poached lobster waiting in my room backstage. I figured I had a few seconds to make a break for the concessions, before the fans filed out. I dashed out the back door, and entered closest food stand.

Carnal Asada. Kick ass. What a cool fucking name. Mexican food in San Diego was always amazing. I was grateful to have my last show here, one of my favorite cities. I slid to the counter to order some tacos, when something besides food whet my appetite.

Jet-black hair that skimmed her back, huge tits that filled out her t-shirt, jeans that hugged her phat ass. Her plump lips were painted pink, but besides that she didn't seem to have a hint of makeup on. Wow— did this woman have any clue how naturally beautiful she was?

She barely looked up from the register. "What can I get for you?"

"I'll have two *carne asada* tacos and your number."

Her head straightened and her eyes met mine, her lashes rapidly blinking. "Oh my god! You're Dax, aren't you? I'm so sorry I didn't notice you there. What are you doing out here? You'll get mobbed."

People starting exploding out of the concert hall, and she was right, I had to get backstage. "It's cool. Bring me my food to my dressing room." I threw down a twenty-dollar bill and handed her a laminated back stage pass.

She brushed her hand through her hair, and rubbed the back of her neck. I winked at her and gave her my signature head nod. Before she could say a word, I disappeared backstage.

I stalked passed my singer, Trey. Motherfucker, tried to shake my hand. Fuck him. Fuck them all. Guy was a dick, always had been. Long time suffered of LSD, Lead Singer Disease. I was honest to god glad to be free of these fuckers, I just wished I could've left on my own terms.

I opened my dressing room, grateful that the bullshit statement about my departure wouldn't be released until tomorrow. Creative differences my ass. But I refused to be a sob story to the media. I had a plan. Tomorrow I would vanish, and I would make my own path. I was twenty-one, I had my whole life ahead of me.

I peeled off my leather pants and hopped into the shower. The hot water scalded my skin, and I scrubbed the concert off of my chest.

I heard a knock at the door. Great—dinner had arrived. And dessert.

"Dax, uhm it's Marisol, from Carnal Asada? I brought your food. I'll just leave it at the table."

Not so fast sweetheart. "Hey, hold up. I'll be out in a second."

I wrapped a towel around my waist, and opened the bathroom door. "Thanks, babe. Hey, what are you doing tonight?"

Her eyes scanned my body, dropping briefly to my cock but then focusing back on my face. "I have to clean up at the restaurant and then I was going to head home."

I walked over to her, careful to maintain eye contact. "No, you're not. You're coming to Vegas with me."

Her jaw dropped, wide enough for me to imagine my cock in it. "Vegas? You're out of your mind. Don't you have groupies or something?"

I laughed. "Groupies bore the fuck out of me. My bandmates are assholes, everyone in my entourage is paid to tell me how fucking awesome I am. I want a good girl who wants to be bad. Are you game?"

Order Now:

The Angel & The Rockstar

ALANA ALBERTSON IS the former President of RWA's Contemporary Romance, Young Adult, and Chick Lit chapters. She holds a M.Ed. from Harvard and a BA in English from Stanford. She lives in San Diego, California, with her husband, two sons, and six rescue dogs. When she's not saving dogs from high kill shelters through her rescue Pugs N Roses, she can be found watching episodes of Cobra Kai, Younger, or Dallas Cowboys Cheerleaders: Making the Team.

Please join my newsletter to receive 2 free books!

Newsletter

Website

Email Me

Facebook Group

ACKNOWLEDGMENTS

I WOULD LIKE to thank my amazing editors on this book:

Kelli Collins who ripped the earlier version apart and helped me reshape the entire thing.

Gwen Hayes who is my arc goddess.

Deborah Halverson, for not giving up on this book and my writing.

To my husband, Roger, a real Marine hero. Thank you for watching the boys while I write and tolerating my endless "what if" conversations about my characters. I couldn't have written this book without you.

To my two beautiful sons, Connor and Caleb. You are both the best part of my day.

To my critique partners:

M-E Girard, for your insightful edits into the characterization of Bret and Selena. You are the reason I won so many contests!

Juliette Sobanet, for all your spot on critiques and guidance. I'm so happy you moved to San Diego!

To my agent, Jill Marsal, for believing in this story in its many different versions.

To my brother, Joe Chulick, for convincing me to publish it. My sister-in-law Susie Chulick, for your uplifting encouragement.

To my mother, Diana Chulick, for fostering my love of reading.

To my three favorite romance writers, Kristan Higgins, Lauren Willig, and Susan Donovan. Thank you for taking your time to give me brilliant critiques on this book.

To all my fellow RWA members, for supporting this book, teaching me how to write, and critiquing this manuscript.

To my brilliant cover designer, Aria Tan. I heart you!